I0833167

Dear Reader,

October is a funny month in New York City. Sometimes it rains, sometimes it snows, sometimes it's sunny. And in the stores, there's the anticipation of Halloween with candy and costumes. Although children don't usually trick-or-treat in my building, I still buy candy and wear a witch's hat just in case. Maybe this year, a group of goblins and vampires will show up so that I won't have to eat a whole bag of chocolate myself. Speaking of vampires, October is a banner month for our readers. We've got enough paranormal and adventure so that you'll want to keep a light on at all times.

New York Times bestselling author Sharon Sala returns to the line with *Rider on Fire* (#1387), which features a biker chick heroine who is led on a mystical journey to her long-lost father. Of course, she finds true love on her quest…and danger. RITA® Award-winning author Catherine Mann continues her popular WINGMEN WARRIORS miniseries with *The Captive's Return* (#1388), where an airman finds his long-lost wife. As they race to escape a crime lord, will they reclaim their passion for each other?

You'll love Ingrid Weaver's *Romancing the Renegade* (#1389), the next book in her PAYBACK miniseries. Here, a sweet bookworm is swept off her feet by a dashing FBI agent, who enlists her aid in the recovery of lost treasure. Make sure to wear your garlic necklace with Caridad Piñeiro's *Temptation Calls* (#1390), in which a beautiful vampire falls for a mortal man. And while she's only known men as abusive, will this dashing detective tempt her out of the darkness? This story is part of Caridad's miniseries THE CALLING.

Have a joyous October and be sure to return next month to Silhouette Intimate Moments, where your thirst for suspense and romance is sure to be satisfied. Happy reading!

Sincerely,

Patience Smith
Associate Senior Editor

Please address questions and book requests to:
Silhouette Reader Service
U.S.: 3010 Walden Ave., P.O. Box 1325, Buffalo, NY 14269
Canadian: P.O. Box 609, Fort Erie, Ont. L2A 5X3

SHARON SALA

Rider on Fire

Silhouette®

INTIMATE MOMENTS™

Published by Silhouette Books

America's Publisher of Contemporary Romance

SILHOUETTE BOOKS

ISBN 0-373-27457-2

RIDER ON FIRE

Copyright © 2005 by Sharon Sala

Visit Silhouette Books at www.eHarlequin.com

Printed in U.S.A.

SHARON SALA

is a child of the country. As a farmer's daughter, she found her vivid imagination made solitude a thing to cherish. During her adult life, she learned to survive by taking things one day at a time. An inveterate dreamer, she yearned to share the stories her imagination created. For Sharon, her dreams have come true, and she claims one of her greatest joys is when her stories become tools for healing.

In addition to her titles for Silhouette, she now writes mainstream novels for MIRA Books under her own name and also as Dinah McCall.

This past month, another member of the Oklahoma Outlaws, our state chapter of Romance Writers of American, was diagnosed with breast cancer. We have less than forty members in the chapter and a half dozen of those are breast cancer survivors. Devastating illnesses are never fair. They didn't get to pick and choose the trials and tribulations that came with living their lives, but by golly those girls know how to live it regardless.

Because I am so proud to be an Outlaw, and because I love and admire those women so much for showing us what's really important in life, I would like to dedicate this book to them.

Ladies, this is my "pink ribbon" for all of you.

To Peggy King, Jo Smith, Willie Ferguson, Julia Mozingo, Chris Rimmer and Donnell Epperson, and to all the women everywhere, including my editor, Leslie Wainger, who have been forged in the fire of cancer and lived to be inspirations for us all—
PINK FOREVER!!!

Chapter 1

The small squirrel was just ready to scold—its little mouth partially opened as it clutched the acorn close to its chest. In the right light, one could almost believe the tail had just twitched.

Franklin Blue Cat called it The Sassy One. It was one of his latest carvings and in three months would be featured, along with thirty other pieces of his work, in a prestigious art gallery in Santa Fe. He hoped he lived long enough to see it.

Franklin often thought how strange the turns his life had taken. Had anyone told him that one day he would become known the world over for his simple carvings, he would have called them crazy. He would also have called them crazy for telling him that, at the age of sixty, he would be alone and dying of cancer. He'd always imagined himself going into old age surrounded by children and grandchildren with a loving wife at his side.

He set aside the squirrel. As he did, the pain he'd been living with for some months took a sharp upward spike, making Franklin reel where he stood. He waited until the worst of it passed, then stumbled to his bedroom and collapsed on his bed.

He considered giving Adam Two Eagles a call. Adam's father had been the clan healer. Everyone had assumed that Adam would follow in his father's footsteps. Only Adam had rebelled. Instead, he had taken the white man's way and left the Kiamichi Mountains to go to college, graduated from Oklahoma State University with an MBA, and from there, gone straight into the army to eventually become one of their elite—an Army Ranger.

Then, during the ensuing years, something had happened to Adam that caused him to quit the military, and brought him home. He'd come back to eastern Oklahoma, to his Kiowa roots, and stepped into his father's footsteps as if he'd never been away.

Adam never talked about what had changed him, but Franklin knew it had been bad. He saw the shadows in Adam's eyes when he thought no one was looking. However, Franklin knew something that Adam did not. Franklin knew it would pass. He'd lived long enough to know life was in a constant state of flux.

As Franklin drifted to sleep, he dreamed, all the way back to his younger days and the woman who'd stolen his heart.

Leila of the laughing eyes and long dark hair. He couldn't remember when he hadn't loved her. They'd made love every chance they could get—with passion, but without caution.

Sleep took him to the day he had learned that Leila's family was moving. She'd been twenty-two to his thirty—

old enough to stay behind. He'd begged her to stay but there had been a look on her face he'd never seen before, and instead of accepting his offer of marriage, she'd been unable to meet his gaze.

His heartbeat accelerated as he relived the panic. In his mind, he could see her face through the back window of the car as her father drove away.

She was crying—his Leila of the laughing eyes was sobbing as she waved goodbye. He could see her mouth moving.

Franklin shifted on the bed. This was new. He didn't remember her calling out. In real life, she'd done nothing but cry as they drove away. It was the way he'd remembered it for all these years. So why had the dream been different? What was it she was trying to say?

He swung his legs to the side of the bed and then stood, giving himself time to decide if he had the strength to move. Finally, he walked out of his bedroom, then through the kitchen to the back porch. The night air was sultry and still.

He stood for a few moments, absorbing the impact of the dream, waiting for understanding. At first, he felt nothing. His mind was blank, but he knew what to do. It was the same thing he always did as he began a new piece of work. All he had to do was look at the block of wood until he saw whatever it was that was waiting to come out. Only then did he begin carving.

Following his instincts, he closed his eyes, took a slow breath, then waited for the words Leila had been trying to say.

It was quiet on the mountain. Almost too quiet. Even the night birds were silent and the coyotes seemed to have gone to ground. There was nothing to distract Franklin from watching his dream, letting it replay in his head. He stood motionless for so long that dew settled on his bare feet, while an owl, feeling no threat, passed silently behind him on its way out to hunt.

And then understanding came, and with it, shock. Franklin turned abruptly and looked back at his house, almost expecting Leila to be on the porch, but there was no one there.

He turned again, this time looking to the trees beyond his home. He'd been born on this land. His parents had died in this house, and soon, so would he. But there was something he knew now that he had not known yesterday.

Leila had taken something of his when she'd left him.

His child.

Right in the middle of his revelation, exhaustion hit.

Damn this cancer.

His legs began to shake and his hands began to tremble. He walked back to the house, stumbling slightly as he stepped up on the porch, then dragged himself into the house.

What if he could find his Leila—even if she was no longer his? He wanted to see their child—no—he *needed* to know that a part of him would live on, even after he was gone. Tomorrow, he would call Adam Two Eagles. Adam would know what to do.

Adam Two Eagles rarely had to stretch to reach anything. At three inches over six feet tall, he usually towered over others. His features were Native American, but less defined than his father's had been. His mother had been Navajo and the mix of Kiowa and Navajo had blended well, making Adam a very handsome man. His dark hair was thick and long, falling far below his shoulders—a far cry from the buzz cut he'd worn in the military. But that seemed so long ago that it might as well have been from another life.

This morning, he was readying himself for a trip up the Kiamichis. There were some plants he wanted for healing that grew only in the higher elevation. It would mean at least a half-day's hike up and back—nothing he hadn't done countless times before—only today, he felt unsettled. He kept going from room to room, thinking there was something else he was supposed to do, but nothing occurred to him. Finally, he'd given up and prepared to leave.

If he hadn't forgotten the bag he liked to carry his herbs and plants in, he would have already been gone when the phone rang. But he was digging through a closet, and ignoring the ring would have been like a doctor ignoring a call for help.

"Hello."

"Adam! I was beginning to think you were gone."

Adam smiled as he recognized the voice.

"Good morning, Franklin. You just caught me. How have you been?"

"The same," Franklin said shortly, unwilling to dwell on his illness. "But that's not why I called."

Adam frowned. The seriousness in his old friend's voice was unfamiliar.

"So, what's up?" Adam asked.

"It's complicated," Franklin said. "Can you come over?"

"Yes, of course. When do you need me?" Adam asked.

There was a moment of hesitation, then Franklin sighed. "Now, I need you to come now."

"I'm on my way," Adam said, and hung up.

In less than fifteen minutes, Adam was pulling up to Franklin's house. He parked, then killed the engine. When he looked up, Franklin had come outside and was waiting for him on the porch. He smiled and then waved Adam up before moving back into the house. Adam bolted up the steps and followed him.

A few minutes were wasted on small talk and the pouring of coffee before Adam urged Franklin to sit down. Franklin did so without arguing. Adam took a seat opposite Franklin's chair and leaned back, waiting for the older man to begin.

"I had a dream," Franklin said.

Adam set his coffee aside and leaned forward, resting his elbows on the arms of his chair.

"Tell me."

Franklin relayed what he'd dreamed, and what he believed that it meant. When he was finished, he leaned back and crossed his arms across his chest.

"So, can you help me?" he asked.

"What do you want me to do?" Adam countered.

Franklin sighed. "I guess, I want to know if I'm right, if Leila and I had a child. I want to know this before I die."

Adam stood, then paced to the window, absently staring at the way sunlight reflected from his windshield onto a wind chime hanging from the porch. He knew what Franklin was asking. He just wasn't convinced Franklin would get the answer he desired.

"So, will you make medicine for me?" Franklin asked.

Adam turned abruptly and asked, "Will you accept what comes, even if it's not what you wanted?"

"Yes."

Adam nodded shortly. "Then, yes, I'll help you."

Franklin sighed, then swiped a shaky hand across his face.

"What do you need from me?" he asked.

"Something that is remarkably yours alone."

Franklin hesitated a moment, then left the room. He returned shortly carrying a carving of an owl in flight.

"This was my first owl. Would this do?"

"Are you willing to sacrifice it?"

Franklin rubbed a hand over the owl one last time, as if imprinting the perfection of the shape and the feathers in his mind, then handed it over.

Adam took it. The wood felt warm where Franklin had been holding it, adding yet another layer of reality to the piece. Then he took out his knife.

"Are you still on blood thinner?" Adam asked.

Franklin nodded.

"Then hair will have to do."

Franklin sat down. Adam deftly separated a couple of strands of Franklin's hair from his head and cut them off, wrapped them in his handkerchief and put them in his pocket.

"Is that all you need?" Franklin asked.

Adam nodded. "I will make medicine for you."

Franklin's shoulders slumped with relief. "When will we know if it worked?"

"When someone comes."

"When? Not if, but when? How can you be so sure?"

"I know what I know," Adam said, and it was all he would say.

For Franklin, it wasn't enough, but it would have to do. "Then I will wait," he said.

Adam nodded, then picked up his coffee cup and leaned back in his chair and took a sip.

Franklin picked up his cup as well, but he didn't drink. He tightened his fingers around the mug, letting the warmth of the crockery settle within him as he watched his old friend's son.

Adam was looking out the window, his eyes narrowing sharply as he squinted against the light. Franklin thought that Adam looked a lot like his father. Same strong face—same far-seeing expression in his eyes, but he was taller and more muscular. And he'd been beyond the Kiamichis. He'd lived a warrior's life for the United States government.

Franklin set his coffee cup aside, folded his hands in his lap, and closed his eyes.

It was good that Adam Two Eagles had come home.

Within an hour after arriving back at his home, Adam began the preparations. He drank some water before going out to ready the sweat lodge. On the way down the hillside, he got work gloves from the tool shed and a small hatchet from a shelf.

A sense of peace came over him as he worked, gathering wood and patching a small hole in the lodge. Tonight, he would begin the ceremony. If Franklin and Leila had made a baby together, the Old Ones would find it.

He hurried back to the house, gathering everything he needed, then walked back to the small lodge above the creek bank.

He undressed with care, shedding his clothes a layer at a time. By the time he'd dropped his last garment, a slight breeze had come up, lifting his hair away from his face and cooling the sweat beading on his body. The first star of the evening was just visible when he looked up at the sky. He checked the fire. Ideally, there would be someone outside the lodge continuing to feed the fire, but not tonight. Tonight the fire that he'd already built would serve the purpose.

He lifted the flap and crawled in. Within seconds, he was covered in sweat. He sat down cross-legged, letting his arms and hands rest on his knees. With a slow, even rhythm he breathed in and breathed out. Then he closed his eyes and began to chant. The words were almost as old as the land on which he sat.

The hours passed and the moon that had been hanging high in the sky, was more than halfway through its slow descent to the horizon. Morning was but an hour or so away.

Inside the sweat lodge, all the words had been said. All the prayers had been prayed.

Adam was ready.

He crawled out of the lodge. When he stood, the muscles in his legs tried to cramp, but he walked them out as he then moved behind the lodge and laid another stick of wood on the fire.

With the sweat drying swiftly on his skin and his mind and body free from impurities, he reached into his pack and took out the carving, as well as the hairs he'd cut from Franklin's head.

Some might have called it a prayer—others might have said it was a chant—but the words Adam spoke were a call to the Old Ones. The rhythm of the syllables rolled off Adam's tongue like a song. The log he'd laid on the fire popped, sending a shower of sparks up into the air. Adam felt the prick of heat from one as it landed on his skin, but he didn't flinch.

Still wrapped in the cloak of darkness, he lifted his arms to the heavens and began to dance. Dust and ashes rose up from the ground, coating his feet and legs as he moved in and out of the shadows around the fire. He danced and he sang until his heartbeat matched the rhythm of his feet.

The wind rose, whistling through the trees in a thin, constant wail, sucking the hair from the back of his neck and then swirling it about his face.

They were coming.

He tossed the owl and the hairs into the fire, and then

lifted his hands above his head. As he did, there was what he could only describe as an absence of air. He could still breathe, but he was unable to move.

The great warriors manifested themselves within the smoke, using it to coat the shapes of what they'd once been. They came mounted on spirit horses with eyes of fire. The horses stomped and reared, inhaling showers of sparks that had been following the column of smoke, and exhaling what appeared to be stars.

One warrior wore a war bonnet so long that it dragged beneath the ghost horse's feet. Another was wrapped in the skin of a bear, with the mark of the claw painted on his chest. The third horse had a black handprint on its flank, while matching handprints of white were on the old warrior's cheeks. The last one rode naked on a horse of pure white. The wrinkles in his face were as many as the rivers of the earth. His gray hair so long that it appeared tangled in the horse's mane and tail, making it difficult to tell where man ended and horse began.

They spoke in unison, with the sounds getting lost in the whirlwind that brought them, and yet Adam knew what they'd said.

They would help.

As he watched, one by one, they reached into the fire and took a piece of Franklin's essence to help them with their search. Then, as suddenly as they'd appeared, they were gone.

Adam dropped to his knees, then passed out.

Chapter 2

DEA agent Sonora Jordan was running after a drug dealer when she fell into the twilight zone. One moment she was inches away from grabbing her perp, Enrique Garcia, and the next her gun went flying as she fell flat on her face. The shot that would have hit her square in the back went flying over her head. Instead of the heat and dust of Mexico, she was in the shade of a forest and hearing the sound of moving water from somewhere up ahead.

She lifted her head, and as she did, she saw a tall, older man standing on the porch of a single-story dwelling that was surrounded by trees. His skin was brown, and his hair was long and peppered with gray. There was a wind chime hanging by his head that looked like a Native American dream catcher. The chimes were different shapes of feathers. It was so foreign to anything she knew, she couldn't

imagine why she would be hallucinating about it and won-
dered if she was dead.

The man lifted his hand, and as he did, she had the
strongest urge to wave back, but she couldn't seem to move.
She couldn't see his face clearly, yet she knew that he was
crying. A sad, empty feeling hit her belly and then swal-
lowed her whole.

By the time she realized she wasn't dead, only face
down in the dirt, the vision was gone. If that wasn't enough
humiliation, her perp was nowhere in sight.

"Oh crap," she muttered, then breathed easier when she
saw Agent Dave Wills coming back with the perp she'd
been chasing. Garcia was handcuffed and cursing at the top
of his voice.

"Can it, Garcia," Wills snapped, then saw Sonora on the
ground. "Jordan! Are you all right? Are you hit?"

"No…no, I'm okay," Sonora said, as she got up, picked
up her gun, then began brushing at the dust on her face and
clothes.

"What happened?" he asked, as he shoved Garcia into
the back of his car and slammed the door.

She didn't know what to say. "I guess I tripped." It was
lame, but it was better than the truth.

He frowned. Sonora Jordan wasn't the tripping kind. He
reached for her shoulder, intent on brushing a streak of dirt
from her face when movement caught the corner of his eye.
He turned just as the other Garcia brother appeared.

"Look out!" he yelled, shoving Sonora aside as he
reached for his gun.

Sonora reacted without thinking. Her gun was still in her
hand and she was falling again. Only this time, she got off
four shots. Two of them connected.

Juanito Garcia died before he hit the ground.

Enrique saw the whole thing from Wills's car, and began to scream, cursing Sonora and Wills and the DEA in general.

Wills waved his arm at another agent and yelled, "Get him out of here!"

As he was being driven away, Enrique looked back at Sonora, mouthing the words, "You're dead."

It wasn't anything she hadn't heard before, but it never failed to give her the creeps.

Wills eyed the muscle jerking in her jaw but shrugged it off. She was tough, no need getting bent out of shape on her behalf. Still, this bust hadn't gone as they'd planned.

"They made you too early," he said. "What happened?"

She spun, eyeing him angrily. "Oh hell, Wills, I hate to venture a guess, but it might have been your ugly mug showing up a good ten minutes too soon. I wasn't through making my play when you came flying around the corner."

Wills shrugged. "But we got 'em."

"No, we got two. Miguel Garcia is the boss man and he wasn't here…yet."

This time Wills frowned. "So, it's not my fault he didn't show. You said he would."

"Yeah…at three-fifteen."

"So, what time is it now?" Wills asked.

"Three-fifteen," Sonora snapped, then strode to her car and got in, slamming the door behind her. When Wills still hadn't moved, she leaned out the window and yelled. "You plan on buying a house down here?"

Wills glanced down at what was left of Juanito Garcia and then at the faces peering out at them from windows above the street.

"Hell no," he said.

Within minutes, they were gone, leaving the aftermath

and cleanup to others. There was a border to cross and reports to be written before anyone slept tonight.

Sonora typed the last word in her report and then hit print. She gathered up the pages with one eye on the clock and the other on the scowl her boss was wearing.

Gerald Mynton wasn't any happier than she'd been about letting Miguel Garcia get away. Capturing two out of three wasn't the kind of odds Mynton operated on. He was an all or nothing kind of man. Added to that, Sonora Jordan was no longer a viable agent in this case. He knew Wills was partly responsible for missing the last Garcia brother, but there was nothing they could do about it now except pick up where they left off—minus Jordan.

When he saw Sonora get up from her desk, he motioned for her to come in. She gathered up what was obviously her report, and strode across the floor.

Even though he was a happily married man and totally insulted by the thought of sexual harassment among his agents, he couldn't ignore what a beautiful woman Sonora was. She was over five-feet-nine inches tall and could bench press double her weight. Her hair was long and dark and her features exotically beautiful. In all the years he'd known her, he'd only seen her smile a few times.

But it wasn't her looks that made her a valuable agent. Besides her skill, there was an asset Sonora had that made her a perfect agent. She had no relatives and no boyfriends. She was as alone in this world as a person could be, which meant that her loyalties were one hundred percent with the job.

Unfortunately, killing Juanito Garcia had temporarily put an end to her usefulness, and until Miguel Garcia was brought to justice, she needed to lay low. Miguel was the kind of man who dealt in revenge.

Gerald Mynton hated to be in corners, but he was in one now. If he put Sonora back to work on anything new, Garcia could dog her until he got a chance to kill her. Mynton's only option was for her to drop out of sight until Garcia was brought in and she could live to solve another case.

He squinted thoughtfully as Sonora entered his office. Now he had to convince her that it was in her best interest to hide, when he knew her instincts would be to confront and overcome.

"My report," Sonora said, as she laid the file on his desk.

He nodded. "Close the door, then please sit down."

Sonora stood her ground with the door wide open. "I'm not hiding."

Mynton sighed. "Did I say you should?"

"Not yet, but you're going to, aren't you?"

"There's a contract out on your life."

Sonora's chin jutted. "I heard."

"So…do you have a death wish?"

"No, but—"

"Garcia won't take what happened without payback. No matter what case I put you on, your presence could put everyone else in danger, not to mention yourself."

Sonora's shoulders slumped. "I hate this."

"I'm not all that excited about it myself," Mynton said.

Sonora nodded. She wasn't the kind of person who let herself be down for long. If this was the way it was going to play out, then so be it.

"I'm sorry, sir. I'll do as you ask," she said.

Mynton stood up and then walked around his desk until they were standing face to face.

"You don't apologize," he said shortly. "You don't ever apologize for doing your job and doing it well. Do you hear me?"

"Yes, sir."

"Is there anyplace special you can go?"

She thought of the hallucination she'd had in Mexico—of the house surrounded by a forest of green and the wind chime hanging on the porch. It had seemed so perfect. If only it had been real, she'd already be there.

"Not really. I'll think of something, though."

"Find a different mode of transportation. We don't think Garcia is in Phoenix yet, but once here, it won't take him long to find out where you live. I don't want you to be there when he arrives. As for leaving Phoenix, you can be traced too easily by credit card. Also, I'd skip the airports and bus stations."

"Well, damn it, sir, since my broom is also in the shop, what the hell else do you suggest?"

Mynton's frown deepened. "Use your imagination."

"This is a nightmare," Sonora muttered. "Just do me one favor."

"If I can," Mynton said.

"Find Miguel Garcia," she added.

"And you stay safe and keep in touch," he added.

A few minutes later, she was gone.

By the time she got home, she was exhausted. However, there were plans to be made. Mynton wanted her to get lost. He didn't know it, but she'd been lost all her life. Dumped on the doorstep of a Texas orphanage when she was only hours old, Sonora had grown up without a sense of who she was or where she was from. When she was young, she used to pretend that her mother would suddenly appear and whisk her away, but it had never happened. Life, for Sonora, was nothing but one kick in the teeth after another. She didn't believe in luck, had never believed in Santa Claus or the Easter Bunny, and trusted no one. What had happened on their last case had been unexpected, but she could handle it. All she needed to do was get out of town.

Transportation was no problem. She knew exactly how she would travel. All she needed to do was call her old boyfriend, Buddy Allen, and have him bring back her Harley.

She stripped down to a bra and panties before she sat down on the side of the bed. She rubbed the back of her neck with both hands, wishing she had time for a massage, but that was too public for someone who needed to lay low.

She picked up the phone and dialed Buddy's number. Although it had been more than six months since they'd quit seeing each other, they were still on good terms. Sonora had been gone too much to commit herself to anyone, and Buddy wanted more than a once a month lay. The decision to quit trying had been mutual.

Still, as she waited for Buddy to pick up, she couldn't help but wish she had a little back-up in her personal life.

Buddy answered on the third ring. "Heelloo, good lookin'."

"Did you know it was me, or is that the way you always answer your phone?" Sonora said.

Buddy laughed. "Caller ID and yes."

This time, it was Sonora who chuckled. "Some things never change…you being one of them," she said.

Buddy sighed. "Did you call to chastize me for being male, or can I talk you into a round of good sex for old times sake?"

"No on both counts. I called because I need my bike."

Buddy groaned. "Aw, man…not the Harley."

"Sorry, but I need it," Sonora said shortly.

The smile disappeared from Buddy's voice. "Are you in trouble?"

"Not if I get out of town quick enough."

"Damn it, Sonora, why do you do it?"

"Do what?" she asked.

"You know what. There are a hundred careers you could have picked besides the one that you chose and none of them would have been dangerous."

"Can you bring it over?" she asked. "I'd come get it, but I don't want to advertise my presence any more than necessary."

Buddy sighed. "Hell yes, I'll bring the Harley, serviced, gassed up and clean. When do you need it?" he asked.

"Yesterday."

Buddy cursed and asked, "Do you need to leave before morning?"

"No. It can wait until then, but early…please."

"Thanks for nothing," he muttered. "I'll be there before seven a.m. Will you make me some coffee?"

"Yes."

"And maybe some of your biscuits and gravy?"

"No."

He sighed. "Can't blame a guy for trying."

"I'm not blaming you for anything," she said. "Never have. Never will."

"I know," Buddy said, and knew that she was no longer talking about the bike. "See you in the morning."

"Okay, Buddy, and thanks."

"It's okay, honey," Buddy said, and hung up.

With that job over, Sonora walked to the closet, then grabbed her travel bag and quickly packed. She thought about where she might go and then went into the living room, found an atlas and carried it to the kitchen.

She opened the pages to the map of the U.S. and then just sat and stared. One line seemed to stand out from all the others. She fumbled in a drawer for a yellow highlighter, then popped the cap. Her fingers where shaking as she held it over the map. Something rattled behind her, like pebbles in a can. She ignored it and began to mark.

Without a thought in her head, she began drawing a line north out of Phoenix toward Flagstaff, then across the country until she came to Oklahoma. The line ended there.

She paused, frowned, then shook her head, certain she'd just lost her mind. Still, she left the atlas on the counter as she went into her bedroom.

She showered quickly, afraid that the vision would come back. Even after she crawled into bed and closed her eyes, she was reluctant to sleep. Finally, she rolled onto her side, bunched her pillow under her neck, then grabbed the extra one and hugged it to her. It was an old habit from childhood, and one she rarely indulged in anymore. The simple act made her feel childish and helpless and Sonora was neither of those.

Somehow she slept, and woke up just after six. Time enough for a quick shower.

True to his promise, Buddy showed up right before seven.

She met him at the door with a to-go cup of coffee.

"Good morning," she said, eyeing his tousled hair and unshaven face. "Thanks for bringing the Harley."

"You're welcome," he said, dropped the keys in her hands, handed her the helmet, and took the coffee, downing a good portion of it before he spoke again. "I don't suppose you'd like to tell me what's going on?"

She shrugged. "Someone wants me dead."

"Sonofabitch," Buddy muttered.

"Yes, he is," Sonora said. "A real bad one. I don't think anyone knows about you and me, but just to be on the safe side, don't mention my name to anyone."

"There is no more you and me," Buddy reminded her.

"And don't worry about me. I'm not the one with the death wish."

Sonora frowned. "I don't have a death wish. I just do my job and do it well." Then she kissed him on the cheek, as much as a thank-you as for old times sake, as well as for bringing back her bike, then pointed at the cab in the street. "I suppose that's your ride. Don't keep him waiting."

She watched him get into the cab before checking the area for someone who didn't belong. All was well. When he looked back, she waved goodbye, then quickly closed the door.

She walked through her home one last time, making sure everything was as it should be, then shouldered her bag, picked up the helmet, and turned off the lights. She opened the door, hesitating briefly to scan the neighborhood once more, and saw nothing amiss. The black and shiny Harley was at the curb.

She hurried outside, opened the storage compartment and dropped her handgun inside, then lowered the lid and tied her bag down on top. When she stuck the key in the ignition, she could tell Buddy had been good for his word. Not only was the bike clean, but the gas gauge registered full. She checked to make sure her toolbox was in place, then put on the helmet and slung her leg over the bike as if she was mounting a horse.

The engine roared to life, then settled down to a soft rumble as she released the kickstand and gave it the gas. As the rumble changed to a full-throttle blast, she put it in gear and rode away without looking back.

It wasn't until she was on the highway that she remembered the path she'd highlighted on the atlas. There was no reason for her to have chosen that direction, and a couple of times she even considered turning around and heading for Las Vegas or points farther west. But something more than instinct was guiding her trip.

Chapter 3

Miguel Garcia was in Juarez, trying to figure out how to get over the border. The Mexican police had staked out his hotel and would have already had him in custody if it hadn't been for Jorge Diaz, one of his dealers, who'd sent his own child into the restaurant where Miguel was having breakfast to warn him.

Now he was in a dingy room over what must be the oldest cantina in the city, without his clothes, and without access to his bank. Even though he hadn't been born to it, Miguel had been in the drug business long enough that he'd become accustomed to fine dining, elegant surroundings. Being forced to hide in a room like this was like a slap in the face—a degradation that only added to the grief of losing his brothers.

Enrique was incarcerated somewhere in the States, and Juanito was on a slab in a Tijuana morgue. He'd promised his mother on her deathbed that he would take care of Juanito. He was the baby of their family, the last of eight children, but now, because of that DEA bitch, Juanito was dead.

Before he'd gone into hiding, Miguel had made a promise at his mother's grave that he would avenge Juanito's death. He'd also let it be known that he would pay big money for the name and location of the agent who'd killed his brother, with the warning to leave her alone. He wanted to end her life—personally.

And so he waited. And waited. A day passed in this hell, then a second, then a third before everything changed.

The *puta* Miguel had just paid for a blow job was in the bathroom brushing her teeth when someone knocked on his door. He reached for his gun, grabbed the woman who was just coming out of the bathroom, and put his finger to his mouth to indicate she be quiet. His grip on her arm was so painful that she stifled a screech and covered her mouth with both hands. Tears ran down her face, but she didn't move.

Once he was satisfied that she understood what he meant, he whispered in her ear. "Ask who is there."

She nodded, then called out as he told her.

There was a long stretch of silence, then a man spoke, "I have news for Miguel."

Miguel recognized the voice of Jorge, the dealer who'd helped him escape. He pulled the woman away from the door, opened it enough to make sure Jorge was alone, and then shoved her out.

"Get lost," he said.

She scurried away, glad to be leaving in one piece.

"Come in," Miguel said.

Jorge nodded quickly, looked over his shoulder, then

stepped inside. He didn't waste time or words. "You wanted the name of the agent who killed your brother."

Miguel's heart skipped a beat. "Yes."

"Her name is Sonora Jordan. She lives in Phoenix, Arizona."

Miguel stifled the urge to clap his hands. This was the best news he'd had in days. "You are sure."

"*Sí, Patron.*"

Miguel put a hand on Jorge's shoulder to explain why he couldn't pay him yet. "They are watching my home and my bank."

Jorge nodded again. No further explanation was needed. "I know," he said, reaching into his pocket for a roll of hundred dollar bills which he handed to Miguel. "For you, Patron, and if you're ready, I can get you across the border tonight."

Miguel was not only surprised, he was shocked. He had greatly underestimated this man's loyalty. "When this is over, you will be greatly rewarded."

Jorge shrugged. "I expect nothing, Patron. It is my honor to help. At eleven o'clock, there will be one knock on your door. The man who comes will take you to a hacienda outside of Juarez where a private plane will be waiting. The pilot has already gotten clearance for his trip, but it does not include landing in Juarez, so the timing will be crucial. You must not be late because he will not wait. Once across the border, he will touch down briefly at a small airstrip outside of Houston. More money and a car will be waiting for you there. The man who brought it has been instructed to stay until he sees that you're safely on the ground."

Miguel threw his arms around Jorge. "*Gracias, Jorge... gracias.* I will never forget this."

Jorge nodded and smiled. *"Vaya con Dios, Patron."* And then he was gone.

Miguel glanced at his watch. It was just after nine. Within two hours, he would be gone from this place and on his way to fulfilling the promise he'd made at his mother's grave.

As soon as Jorge reached the street, he took out his cell phone and made a call. "Tony, this is Jorge Diaz. I need you to do something for me."

Tony Freely was one of Jorge's mules. He traveled back and forth regularly from his ranch outside of Houston to Juarez, doing his part to make sure that the drug market continued to thrive, and being nicely reimbursed for his troubles.

"Yeah, sure, Jorge. Just name it."

"You remember the old runway where I had you pick up a load about three months back?"

"Yeah, but I thought you didn't want to use it anymore."

"I don't. It's something else," Jorge said. "What I want you to do is go to that runway at an hour before midnight tonight and wait for a small plane to land there. A man will get off. You let him see you. Let him see your face, but don't talk to him. Just get in your car and drive away."

Tony frowned. This didn't sound right, but he knew better than to question Jorge.

"Sure. No problem."

"Thank you," Jorge said. "I'll make it worth your while."

Tony's frown disappeared. Money talked loud and clear to him. "Consider it done," he said, and hung up the phone.

Jorge did the same, smiling as he disconnected. Before he was through, the Garcia brothers' reign of power would be over and he would be the one in charge.

* * *

As promised, Miguel's ride appeared on time. He didn't recognize the short, fat man who came to get him, and the man didn't offer a name. They got to the airstrip without incident. Soon, the lights of Juarez were swiftly disappearing below them. Miguel was already making plans as to how to find Sonora Jordan and make her pay for the death of his brother.

In about an hour, the plane began to lose altitude and Miguel's heartbeat accelerated. He leaned over and peered out the window to the sea of lights that was Houston.

The pilot banked suddenly to the west and began descending. Minutes later, the small plane landed, taking a couple of hard bounces before rolling to an easy stop.

Miguel saw a small hangar and a man standing beneath a single light mounted above the door. In the shadows nearby, he could see the outline of a car.

He owed Jorge big time.

"You get out now," the pilot said shortly.

Miguel frowned. It was the most the man had said to him since they took off. Still, he grabbed his bag and jumped out of the plane. Even as he was walking away, the plane turned around and took off the same way it had landed.

Caught in the back-draft, Miguel ducked his head and closed his eyes while dust and grit swirled around him. When he opened his eyes, the plane was off the ground and the man he'd seen under the lights was gone.

The unexpected solitude and quiet made him a little uneasy, and when a chorus of coyotes suddenly tuned up from somewhere beyond the hangar, he headed for the car on the run.

Only after he was inside with the doors locked and his

hand on the keys dangling from the ignition, did he relax. He started the engine and checked the gauges. The car was full of gas, two maps were on the seat beside him—one of Texas and one of Arizona. After a quick check of the brief-case in the passenger seat, he knew he would have plenty of money to do what had to be done. He backed away from the hangar and followed the dirt road until he hit blacktop. Gauging his directions by the digital compass on the rear-view mirror, he turned north and drove until daylight. The first town he came to, he stopped and ate breakfast, then got a room at the local motel. It was ten minutes after nine in the morning when he crawled between the sheets. Within seconds, he was out.

Even though Sonora had started out with an indefinite direction in mind, the farther she went, the more certain she became that, whatever her future held, she would find it somewhere east.

Near the Arizona border, it started to rain. Sonora stopped and took a room at a chain motel. She tossed her bag onto the bed before heading to the restaurant on site.

Once she finished her meal she started back to her room on the second floor. She was halfway up the stairs when she pulled an Alice and, once again, fell down the rabbit hole.

It was raining. The kind of rain that some people called a toad-strangler—a hard, pounding downpour with little to no wind. She'd never stood in the rain and not been wet before. It was an eerie sensation. And it was night again. Why did insanity keep yanking her around in the dark? It was bad enough she was hallucinating.

She didn't have to look twice to know that she was back at the Native American man's house. Water was running off the roof and down between her feet, following the slope of the ground. All of a sudden, lightning struck with a loud, frightening crack. She flinched, then relaxed. There was no need to panic. She wasn't really here. This was just a dream.

She looked toward the house, then felt herself moving closer, although she knew for a fact that her feet never shifted. Now she was standing beneath the porch and looking into the window. At first, she saw nothing. Then she saw the Native American man lying on the floor near a doorway.

She gasped and started toward the door when she realized that, again, she had no power here. She was nothing but a witness. Dread hit her belly high. Why was she seeing this if she could do nothing about it?

Then, as she was watching through the window, she realized there was a light in the window that hadn't been there before. It took a few moments before she could tell it was a reflection from a vehicle coming down the driveway behind her.

She turned, wanting to call out—willing herself to scream out, please hurry, but as before, she was nothing but an observer.

Adam Two Eagles drove recklessly through the storm. The phone call he'd gotten a short time ago from Franklin had frightened him. Even now as he was turning up Franklin's driveway, the knot in his gut tightened.

Franklin had sounded confused—even fatalistic. Adam didn't think Franklin would do anything crazy, like do himself in, but he couldn't be sure. And when he'd tried to call him back, there had been no answer.

He could have called an ambulance. The people in Broken Bow knew Franklin. They knew he had leukemia. They would send an ambulance, but if it was unwarranted—if Adam had misread the situation—it would embarrass Franklin, and that he didn't want to do. So here he was, driving like a madman in the dark, pouring rain, just to make sure his friend was still of this earth.

As he came around the curve, he saw that the lights were still on in Franklin's house. That was good. At least he wouldn't be waking him up to make sure he was okay.

Lightning struck a tree about a hundred yards in front of him. Even in the rain, sparks flew. Right before the flash disappeared, Adam saw branches exploding, then flying through the air. He swerved as one flew past the hood of his truck, then sped past the site just before the tree burst into flames. It wouldn't burn long in this downpour, but the sooner Adam got out of this rain, the better off he would feel.

He slid to a halt near the porch, jumped out on the run, vaulted up the steps, and had his fist ready to knock when he realized he wasn't alone. He let his hand drop as he slowly turned, staring down the length of the porch to the small square of light coming through the window from inside.

The porch was empty, yet he knew he was being watched. Drawn by an urge he couldn't explain, he moved forward, and when he reached the window, stared out into the night, into the curtain of rain.

"Who's there?" he called, and then for a reason he couldn't explain, reached out and touched the air in front of him.

No one answered, and he felt only the rain.

Shrugging off the feeling as nothing but nerves, he turned back toward the door, and as he did, glanced through the window. Within seconds, he'd spied Franklin's body lying on the floor.

"Oh no," he cried, and ran to the door.

It was locked, but not for long.

Adam kicked the door inward, then ran to his friend.

Sonora's heart was pounding so hard she thought it would burst. Every breath she took was painful, and she felt like she was going to be sick.

The man who'd come out of the storm onto the porch was unbelievable—like some knight in shining armor she might have conjured up during her teenage years.

His skin was the color of burnished copper. His hair was long, black and plastered to his head and neck from the storm. He was tall and lean, without an ounce of fat on him—a fact made obvious by the wet clothes molded to his body. But it was his face that intrigued her. His nose was hawk-like, his chin stubborn and strong. His lips were full and his eyes were dark and impossible to read.

And he was looking straight at her.

Sonora shivered.

This wasn't supposed to be happening.

He wasn't part of the dream.

And it was a dream. It had to be.

When he started toward her, she screamed, or at least she thought she screamed. The sound was going off inside her head like the bells of an alarm, but the man kept coming.

All of a sudden, she fell off the porch. When she came to, she was on her hands and knees on the stairs of the motel.

"Hey, lady! Are you okay? I saw you trip and fall but I was all the way down at the end of the walkway. Couldn't get here fast enough to do you much good."

Sonora shuddered, then brushed at the knees of her pants, and dusted off her hands as she looked up at the man standing at the head of the stairs. He was short and stocky with a bald head and a red beard. An odd combination of features for the guy, but he seemed harmless.

"I'm okay," she said. "I guess I wasn't paying attention to where I was going. I'm fine, but thanks."

The guy nodded, then took a couple steps backward before turning around and going back down the hall to his room.

Sonora unlocked her door and went inside, hung a Do Not Disturb sign on the outside of the doorknob, and then carefully locked the doors. It took even less time to undress, and moments later, fell into bed.

The hallucination she'd just had was still in her mind, but she shrugged it off. She couldn't be bothered with worrying about some stupid daydream with Miguel Garcia still on the loose. With those thoughts in her mind, she fell asleep.

Chapter 4

Sonora crossed the Arizona border into New Mexico just before noon the next day. Traffic was already thicker on I-40, as well as on the access roads. A digital message on a bank near the interstate gave a temperature reading of ninety-eight degrees. With the amount of traffic and exhaust fumes heating up the pavement, Sonora could add another ten degrees of heat to that reading and know she wasn't off by much.

She'd already made a decision that traveling in the heat of the day in this part of the country wasn't smart. So she took the next exit off the interstate and found a motel.

Within minutes she had a room on the ground floor. She left the office and rode her bike to the parking place in front of her room. When she dismounted, she realized her hands and legs were shaking. Too much heat and not enough water, but she was about to fix that. She locked up her bike, shouldered her bag, and unlocked the door to her room, gratefully inhaling the artificially cooled air inside as she entered.

She went to the bathroom to wash up and drank a big glass of water while she was there. There was a café on the other side of the parking lot, which she planned to visit, but not in this hot biker leather. When she came out of the bathroom, she took off her pants and vest, tossed her shirt aside as well as her biker boots for some cooler clothes and tennis shoes.

She stretched and then bounced once on the bed, testing it for comfort. She scooted all the way up on the mattress, then stretched out—but only for a minute. She noticed the red LED light on the smoke detector was working and closed her eyes.

When she woke up, it was after ten p.m. She groaned as she rolled over and swung her legs off the bed.

"Oh great, I didn't mean to sleep so long."

She stood up and went to the window. It was pouring. She probably wouldn't sleep tonight, but she could eat, and her belly was protesting the fact that she hadn't eaten since breakfast.

Grabbing a clean T-shirt and jeans from her bag, she dressed quickly and slipped her wallet in a fanny pack before she left.

Despite the rain, the smell of charcoal and cooking meat was heavy in the air. Her mouth watered as she made a dash across the parking lot and into the café.

"Ooh, honey, come in out of that rain," the hostess said, as Sonora dashed inside. "Are you by yourself?" she added.

Sonora nodded.

The hostess picked up a menu. "This way," she said, and led the way across the floor to a booth in the back. "This okay?"

"Perfect," Sonora said, and meant it. Being at the far end of the room with a clear view of the door was a good thing. The fact that she was close to the kitchen didn't bother her. She wasn't looking for ambiance, just food.

She ordered iced tea, salad and chicken alfredo, then opened a package of crackers and began nibbling on them while she waited for her food to arrive. Lightning flashed outside, momentarily lighting the parking lot. Lights flickered, then went out. A communal groan of dismay sounded throughout the seating area while cursing could be heard in the kitchen.

Sonora automatically felt for her fanny pack, making sure her wallet was in place. Before she could relax, there was the sound of falling furniture, then a woman's shrill scream.

"Help! Help! Someone just stole my purse!"

Sonora was on her feet without thinking. She heard running footsteps coming toward her. The way she figured it, the only person running in the dark would be the perp.

She moved instinctively and heard, more than saw, him coming. What she did see was that the shadow coming toward her was well over six feet tall. Using one of her kickboxing moves, she caught the running man belly high. She heard him grunt, then heard him stagger into a table and some chairs. She spun on one foot and came back around with another kick that caught him in the chest and ended up on his chin.

He went down like a felled ox.

Lights flickered, then fully came on as power was restored.

The woman who'd been robbed was still screaming and crying.

The hostess who'd seated Sonora saw the man on the

floor, then eyed the tall, dark woman she'd just put in the back of the room and pointed. "Lord have mercy, honey! Did you do that?"

"Call the cops," Sonora said.

The man on the floor moaned and started to roll over.

Sonora put her foot in the middle of the man's back and pushed. "Hunh uh," she warned. "You stay right where you are, buddy, or I'll snap your spine faster than you can blink."

"Damn, lady. My belly hurts bad. I think you broke my ribs." The man moaned.

Soon, the squall of approaching sirens could be heard. The perp moaned again.

The police came in the door, followed by a pair of EMTs.

The hostess waved them over. "Here! He's here!" she yelled.

Sonora quickly exited the café through the kitchen, looking wistfully at the food as she ran through. The last thing she needed was to call attention to herself, and she'd done that big time by stopping the perp. The police would have wanted to see her name and ID. Having them identify her as DEA was completely opposite to what she was trying to do—which was get lost.

She hunched her shoulders against the rain and walked out into the parking lot. Quickly, she crossed the street to a pizza place on the corner.

"One more time," she muttered, as she hurried inside.

"Sit anywhere," a waitress said, as she hurried by with an order. "I'll be right with you."

This time, Sonora settled in at a booth near the front door and then leaned her head against the glass as she looked out into the night. She was alternating between sausage or mushroom pizza when another flash of lightning sent her back into the black hole that had become part of her mind.

***

*The older Native American man was sitting at a table
with his back to Sonora. She wanted to go around him and
see what he was doing, but found herself unable to move.*

"Why am I here? What the hell do you want," she yelled.

Either he didn't hear her, or he was ignoring her.

*The man stood up slowly, then walked away, revealing
a small piece of wood and pile of wood curls.*

*He was carving something, but whatever it was, it was
little more than an outline in the wood. Her gaze slid from
the wood to the man. He was shaking pills from a bottle
into his hand. There was a strange expression on his face
as he tossed them down the back of his throat and chased
them with water.*

He's dying.

*The moment Sonora thought it, she flinched. A deep
sadness came over her. "What am I supposed to do?" she
cried. "Why are you haunting me?"*

"Hey, lady!"

Sonora jerked.

"What?"

"I asked you...what do you want?"

Sonora blinked. Traveling from insanity to the real
world was confusing, but she was getting better at it. It
didn't take her but a moment to answer.

"A medium sausage and mushroom pizza and a large
Pepsi."

The waitress nodded and left Sonora on her own again,
only this time, Sonora focused her interests on the people
at the other tables as she waited for her food to arrive.

She was both frustrated and confused by these recurring
hallucinations. Talking to a shrink was a possibility and

probably wise, but she wouldn't risk it. The first time the precinct got wind of an agent in "therapy," that agent would wind up doing desk duty until pronounced fit for duty again. Sonora didn't want that on her record, so she was relying on instinct to get her through this. She couldn't help but feel as if she was seeing this man for a reason. Maybe if he was real, and maybe if she found him, she'd discover for herself what this all meant.

Then the waitress came, delivered the pizza, refilled Sonora's drink and left her to dine alone. By the time she had finished eating and paid for her meal, the rain had stopped. Reflections from the street lights were mirrored in the puddles as she crossed the street to get to her room.

She was wide-awake and itching to be on the move. Despite an old fear of the dark, she handled it better outside. When she thought about it, which was rarely, it always made sense. She'd gotten her fear of the dark from being locked in a closet, so if she wasn't bound by four walls, the fear never quite manifested into a full-blown panic attack. Glad to be on the move again, she packed her bag quickly, dropped her room key off at the office, and mounted up. Within the hour, she was gone.

Miguel Garcia had been in Phoenix less than six hours when he'd gotten his first good lead on Sonora Jordan's whereabouts. He had a name and an address, only it wasn't Sonora's address. It belonged to her ex-boyfriend, Buddy Allen.

It was just after 10:00 p.m. when Buddy pulled into the driveway of his apartment building. It was the first time he'd been home since this morning when he'd left for work. With his mind on a shower and bed, he got off the elevator, carrying a six-pack of beer and a bag of groceries. He set down the six-pack, then toed it into his apartment after he opened the door. The door locked as it swung shut. Buddy was halfway across the living room when it dawned on him that all the lights were on, but he distinctly remembered turning them off when he'd left.

The hair rose on the back of his arms. He set down the sack and the six-pack and stepped backward, intent on leaving the apartment to call the police.

Then a man walked out of the bedroom holding a gun. "You're not going anywhere," he said, and motioned for Buddy to sit down on the sofa.

Buddy measured the distance to the door against the gun and cursed silently. The man didn't look like the kind to be making idle threats.

"Who the hell are you?" Buddy asked.

"My name is of no importance," he said.

"Then what are you doing here?" Buddy countered.

"Looking for a friend of yours."

"Who?" Buddy asked.

"Sonora Jordan."

Buddy's stomach rolled. Suddenly, it hit him how much danger he was in. Sonora didn't deal with lightweights and she'd been spooked enough to leave Phoenix. There was every possibility that he might not live to see another day.

"I don't know where she is," Buddy said.

The man frowned. "Wrong answer," he said, and swung the butt of his gun up under Buddy's chin.

Buddy dropped, then didn't move.

DEA agent Gerald Mynton was pouring his second cup of coffee of the day when the phone rang. He set down his cup and reached across the desk to answer it. "Mynton."

"Agent Mynton, I'm Detective Broyles with Phoenix Homicide."

"Detective, what can I do for you?" Mynton asked.

"I'm not sure, but we're working a murder and the name of one of your agents came up."

Mynton frowned. "Who?"

"Sonora Jordan."

Mynton sat down in his chair with a thump. "What about her?"

"Do you know a man by the name of Robert Allen…goes by the name of Buddy?"

"Not that I—wait! Did you say Buddy Allen?"

"Yes."

"Oh hell," Mynton said.

"Then you do know him?" Broyles asked.

"Not personally, but I do know that Agent Jordan used to date a Buddy Allen. Is he the one who's dead?"

"Yes."

"And you say it was murder?"

"Beat all to hell and back," Broyles said. "Died in E.R. about two hours ago."

"And you're looking for Agent Jordan because?"

"Mr. Allen had a message for her. It was the last thing he said before he died. He said to tell her that, 'he didn't tell.' Do you know what that means?"

Mynton felt sick. "Maybe. Do you have any leads?"

Broyles shuffled his notes.

"Uh…here's what we know so far. Around two in the morning, a neighbor was coming home when she saw a stranger get out of the elevator and leave the building. She said he had blood on the front of his clothes. She got into her apartment and went to bed. But she said she couldn't sleep because she kept hearing an intermittent thump from the apartment above her. She knew it belonged to Buddy Allen, and said it wasn't like him to make noise of any kind, so she called the super. He went up and checked…found Mr. Allen in a pool of blood and called an ambulance. When he died, we were called in. After questioning the other occupants of the building, we're leaning toward the theory that the man the neighbor saw might be our man."

"Got a name?" Mynton asked.

"No, just a description."

"Was he Latino?"

There was a long moment of silence, then Broyles spoke, "Yes, and I want to know how you know that."

"We got word a few days ago that there was a hit out on Agent Jordan." Mynton sighed. "God…we never thought about warning any of her friends. She's going to be sick about this."

"That's all fine, but I want to know about the Latino."

"Of course," Mynton said. "I can't guarantee that the man who killed Allen is the one who's after Sonora Jordan, but just in case…you might be looking for a man named Miguel Garcia, or one of his hired goons."

"We would like to talk to Ms. Jordan."

"Yeah, so would I, but she's gone," Mynton said.

"What do you mean, gone?"

"We knew Garcia was after her. I told her to get lost for a while, but I haven't heard anything from her since she left."

"How long ago was that?"

"Uh…three, maybe four days, I'm not sure."

"Do you have a cell phone number?"

"Yes, but would you allow me to get in contact with her first? She's going to take the news about Allen hard. She'll blame herself for his death and she's already under a load."

"Yes, all right," Broyles said. "But as soon as you contact her, please have her call us."

"Will do," Mynton said.

He hung up the phone, then flipped through his Rolodex for Sonora's cell phone number.

By noon, Mynton had left three messages on Sonora's cell without receiving a call back. He was worried and frustrated by his inability to reach her, but he knew that, if she was okay, she would eventually return his call. It was fifteen minutes to one when he left the office for a lunch meeting.

After riding all night and stopping for a few hours at a motel, it was close to sunset when Sonora mounted the Harley and got back on the road. The setting sun was at her back as she rolled out onto the interstate.

The night promised to be clear. The first star of evening was already out and although the air was swiftly cooling, the heat of the pavement was still a force with which to be reckoned.

The power of the Harley carried Sonora swiftly down the highway. She rode with the confidence of a seasoned biker. Just before the last of the light faded away, Sonora signaled to change lanes, then glanced in the rearview mirror. The last thing she expected to see was the outline of a horse and rider up in the sky, following at her back.

Startled by the sight, the bike swerved slightly. She quickly regained control and then ventured another glance. This time, she saw nothing but a scattering of clouds.

Rattled, she curled her fingers tighter around the handlebars and focused on the road ahead.

It was nothing but clouds in an odd formation—no way had she seen a ghost rider.

No way, indeed.

Miguel Garcia was ticked off. He'd beaten Buddy Allen senseless and still wasn't any better off than he'd been when he'd walked into the apartment. Either the man didn't know, or he'd rather die than tell where Sonora Jordan had gone. All he'd gotten from his visit to Allen's apartment was a photo of Sonora. He'd seen her driver's license photo, but it did not hold a candle to the one Buddy had in a frame. Miguel stared at the image, eyeing the copper-colored skin and straight black hair. Her eyes were dark and almond shaped, her lips full with a twist that could be read as sensual or sarcastic.

Miguel had to admit that Sonora Jordan was beautiful. But beautiful or not, she'd killed Juanito and helped put Enrique in prison and for that she would pay.

Before he'd left the neighborhood, he'd done a little investigating, spread a little money around, and learned that Buddy Allen used to have a Harley parked near his pickup truck, but that he'd ridden away on it about five days ago and come back in a cab. After that, he'd drawn a blank.

Once he got back to his hotel room, Miguel made a call to Jorge Diaz to see if he had any contacts in Phoenix who could hack into computer systems. Jorge had given him a name. Toke Hopper. It turned out to be a good one.

At Miguel's instructions, Toke hacked into the Arizona DMV and discovered that the missing Harley actually belonged to Sonora Jordan, not Robert Allen.

Since Miguel had already been to her apartment and seen the amount of accumulating mail dropped through the slot in her door, he was guessing that she'd already been gone for a few days. He'd been puzzled by the fact that her car was still in its parking place, and assumed she'd taken a plane or a bus out of Phoenix.

Just to make sure his guess had been right, he had Toke check the passenger lists of airlines and buses for the past week. To his surprise, Sonora Jordan had not used either to leave the city. The only thing missing besides Sonora, herself, was the Harley. If she left town on it, he had no way of knowing a destination.

He decided to go back to her apartment and look again. Maybe he'd missed something before that would make sense to him now.

He paid off the hacker and drove back to Sonora's apartment building, then walked in like he owned the place. It was a quarter to eleven in the morning and most of the residents were at work. No one challenged him as he rode the elevator up to her floor and picked the lock on her door as he'd done before.

Once inside, he began going through papers, looking for something—anything—that would give him a clue as to where she'd gone. Thirty minutes later he was no closer to an answer than he had been when he came in, and was ready to give up. He was on his way out of the kitchen when he accidentally dropped his car keys. As he was picking them up, he noticed something on the floor underneath the island. He got down on his hands and knees and pulled it out.

It was nothing but a book. He had a difficult time speaking English and couldn't read it at all, so he was definitely disappointed. He didn't get interested until he realized the book wasn't just a book, it was an atlas—a book of maps.

He was looking for a woman who'd obviously gone on a trip, so he started at the beginning and began turning pages one by one. About six pages in, he came to the page showing the map of the United States and found his first clue.

Someone had taken a highlighter and traced a path north out of Phoenix and into Oklahoma. The yellow line ended near a small town on the interstate called Henryetta.

He didn't know how old the atlas was, or if the yellow line was from a previous trip, but it was simple enough to check out. Within minutes he was gone.

He made Flagstaff around four o'clock and immediately began flashing her picture around at gas stations and eating establishments. It took a couple of hours before he hit pay-dirt.

He found an employee at a gas station who remembered a pretty woman wearing black leather and riding a Harley. When Miguel showed him Sonora's picture, he confirmed it was her that he'd seen.

Miguel was congratulating himself on his detective work and thought about driving on through the night, but when he saw the gathering thunderstorms, he changed his mind. He got a room for the night and settled in, satisfied that he was on the right track.

Sonora was still rattled by her latest hallucination as she rode through Amarillo, Texas, but kept going.

She never knew when she crossed the Oklahoma border, but when the sun finally came up, she saw a sign on the side of the road indicating Clinton and Weatherford were only a few miles ahead. She'd never heard of Clinton, but for some reason, she knew Weatherford was in Oklahoma.

Just knowing that she was in the state fueled a sense of urgency she didn't understand, but she was too weary to go any farther until she'd gotten some food and some sleep.

* * *

Adam Two Eagles had watched the sun rise, then fed his cat before making himself sit down and write checks to pay his bills. Some time today he was going to have to go into town and get groceries, but not for a while. The day was too nice to waste and he'd promised some families he'd go visit and make medicine for them.

And so the day passed as Adam made visits and answered a couple of phone calls for help from his cell phone. He worked without thought of what waited for him back home until it was getting late and he had yet to go to town and get his groceries. In a few hours it would be dark. He thought about waiting until tomorrow to go shopping and started to go inside his house, when suddenly, the front door swung shut in front of him.

Startled, he stopped, opened it, then stood on the threshold and waited, expecting to feel a draft from an open window somewhere in the house.

He felt nothing.

The skin crawled on the back of his neck.

He turned and looked toward the horizon.

The sense of imminency was still with him.

"Okay," he said softly. "I will go to town."

Chapter 5

A man was in the motel parking lot cursing the flat he'd found on his car as a police siren sounded a few blocks over.

Sonora heard none of it. The air conditioning unit near her bed was a buffer against the heat outside, as well as the noise. She slept deeply and without moving, until she began to dream.

She was surrounded by trees. The wind was rustling the leaves overhead. In the distance, she could hear coyotes. She was lost, and yet she wasn't afraid. Something flew past her—most likely an owl. They were night-hunters—like her. As soon as she thought that, she frowned. Why had she referred to herself as a night-hunter? That made no sense.

A twig snapped off to her right.

Sonora froze. Something—or someone—was out there.

"Who's there?" she asked, and then feared the answer.

Another twig snapped. This time from behind her. She wanted to turn around, but as always, she couldn't move.

"Stop it," she yelled. "Either speak up or get the hell away from me. This isn't funny!"

Wind lifted the hair from the back of her neck as she curled her fingers into fists. It took a few moments for it to sink in that the gust of wind was past, but that her hair was still up.

She heard a sigh, then felt something brush the skin above her collar.

"No, no, no," she moaned. "I want to wake up."

"Not yet," someone whispered.

Sonora shuddered.

"Sssh, pretty woman…you are safe."

"Oh God, oh God, I need this to stop. I'm waking up now. Do you hear me? I'm waking up now!"

She closed her eyes, counted to ten, and then opened them, expecting to be anywhere but in a forest, in the dark, with a stranger at her back.

"Why am I not awake?" she moaned.

"Because we are not done," he said softly.

"Then show yourself, damn it!"

There was a long moment of silence. Sonora waited— uncertain what would happen first. Either he would disappear, or she would wake up. Then suddenly, her hair was laying against her neck once more, and she thought she heard him whisper something near her ear. She wasn't sure. It could have been the wind, but she thought she heard him say, "as you wish."

She closed her eyes.

"Look at me."

Panic hit her like a blow to the gut. Be careful of what you ask for, she thought.

"Woman. Look. At. Me."

His voice was firm, but she was no longer afraid.

She took a deep breath and then opened her eyes just as a cloud blew over the moon. In the dark, all she could see were his eyes, looking down at her and glittering like a wolf.

So he was tall.

She felt his breath upon her face, or maybe it was just the wind.

"Do you see me?" he asked.

The wind blew the last of the cloud away from the face of the moon, and he was revealed to her in the moonlight.

It was a stunning face—a face that appeared to have been carved out of rock—all angles and hard planes—except for his mouth. It was full and curved in just a hint of a smile. When he saw that she was looking at his lips, she saw his nostrils flare.

"I see you," she said.

"Then come to me," he demanded.

Sonora woke up just as someone fell against the outside door of her motel room. She heard a burst of muffled laughter and then the sounds faded away.

"Oh God, what is happening to me?" she whispered. "Am I going insane?"

She swung her legs over the side of the bed and looked for the digital clock. It was either broken or unplugged, because the digital readout was dark. She turned on a light, then glanced around for her watch. She didn't see it, tried to remember when she'd looked at it last and failed.

"Great," she muttered, then stumbled to the window. It was still daylight outside.

She glanced back at the bed and then frowned. There

was no way she was going back to bed and chance resuming that dream. It was too unsettling. Without giving herself time to rethink the decision, she hurried to the bathroom. The sooner she got cleaned up and dressed, the sooner she could leave.

She didn't know for sure where she was going, but that hadn't stopped her yet. If she admitted the truth, she hadn't been in control of her life since that day in Tijuana when she'd fallen flat on her face and into what she could only describe as a parallel world. From the time she'd left Phoenix, to right now in this strange motel room in a state named for the Native American Indians who peopled it, she been led by something more powerful than anything she'd ever known before. As confused as she felt, she had come to believe that something—or someone would continue to lead her in the right direction.

As she was dressing, she remembered she'd been going to call her boss. She took the phone off the charger and made the call to the Arizona headquarters of the DEA, but when she was put through to Mynton's office, he was gone. Frustrated, she left him a message saying that she was okay and she'd call him later.

Within an hour, she was back on the Harley with the sun at her back, trusting in a force she could not see.

Franklin Blue Cat was asleep in his favorite lounge chair on the back porch. The disease he was battling and the medications he was taking to fight it often left his body feeling chilled and old beyond his years. Shaded from the sun, and with the breeze in his face, he reveled in the heat of summer.

Although he was still, his sleep was restless, as if his mind refused to waste what little time he had left. In the middle of a breath, pain plowed through his body, bringing him to an immediate upright position and gasping for air. He struggled against panic, wondering if he would be afraid like this when his last breath had come and gone, then shoved the thought aside.

He believed in a higher power and he believed that when his body quit, his spirit did not. It was enough.

He glanced at his work in progress and then pushed himself up from the chair. For whatever odd reason, he had a compulsion to finish this piece before he was too weak to work.

Once up, he decided to get something to drink before he resumed carving. He was in the kitchen when he heard a commotion outside in the front yard. He hurried onto the porch. At first, he saw nothing, although he still heard the sound. Puzzled, he stepped off the porch, then looked up.

High above the house, an eagle was circling. Every now and then it would let out a cry, and each time it did, it raised goosebumps on Franklin's arms.

"I see you, brother," Franklin said.

The eagle seemed to dip his wings, as if to answer, *I see you, too.*

Franklin shaded his eyes with his hand, watching in disbelief as the eagle flew lower and lower.

Was this it? Was this how it would happen? Brother Eagle would come down and take his spirit back to the heavens?

His heart began to pound. His knees began to shake.

Lower and lower, the eagle flew, still circling—still giving out the occasional, intermittent cry. And each time it cried out, Franklin assured Brother Eagle that he was seen.

Franklin didn't realize that he'd been holding his breath until the eagle suddenly folded its wings against its body and began to plummet.

Down, down, down, it came, like a meteor falling to earth.

Franklin couldn't move as the great bird came toward him at unbelievable speed. Just when he thought there was no way they would not collide, the eagle opened his wings, leveled off his flight and sailed straight past Franklin with amazing grace.

Franklin felt the wind from the wings against his face— saw the golden glint of the eagle's eye—and knew without being told that the Old Ones had sent him a sign.

Staggered by the shock of what had just happened, Franklin took two steps backward, then sat down. The dirt was warm against his palms. A ladybug flew, then lit on the collar of his shirt.

He smelled the earth.

He felt the sun.

He heard the wind.

He saw the eagle fly straight up into the air and disappear.

It was then he knew. A change was coming. He didn't know how it would be manifested, but he knew that it would be.

Gerald Mynton got back in the office around three in the afternoon. When he heard Sonora's voice on the answering machine, he groaned. He needed to talk to her and she'd given him no idea whatsoever of where she was or how she could be reached. It was obvious to Mynton that she kept her phone turned off unless she was physically using it, and had to be satisfied with leaving her another message that it was urgent he talk to her. All he could do was hope she called in again soon.

* * *

Sonora passed through Oklahoma City in a haze of heat and fumes from the exhausts of passing trucks and cars. Sweat poured from her hair and into her eyes until she could no longer bear the sting. She pulled over to the shoulder of the road long enough to take off her helmet and get a drink. She emptied a bottle of water that had long since lost its chill, then tossed it back into her pack to be discarded later.

There was some wind, but it did nothing to cool her body against the mid-summer heat of Oklahoma. In the distance, she could see storm clouds building on the horizon and guessed that it might rain before morning. Maybe it was just as well that she'd taken to the highway this day. She knew Oklahoma weather had a predilection for tornadoes. Riding tonight would probably not be a good idea.

Reluctantly, she replaced the helmet, swung the Harley back into traffic, and resumed her eastward trek, passing Oklahoma City, then the exit road to Choctaw, and then exits to Harrah and then Shawnee. It dawned on her as she continued her race with the heat, that nearly every other town she passed had some sort of connection with the Native American Indians.

It wasn't until she came up on Henryetta, once a coal mining town, and now a town claiming rights to being the home of World Champion Cowboys, Troy Aikman and Jim Shoulders, that she felt something go wrong.

She flew past an exit marked Indian Nation Turnpike. Within seconds after passing it, a car came out of nowhere and cut in front of her so quickly that she almost wrecked. It took a few moments for her to get the Harley under control, and when she did, pulled off the highway onto the shoulder of the road.

Her heart was hammering against her chest and she was drenched in sweat inside the leather she was wearing. She sat until she could breathe, without thinking she was going to throw up, and got off the bike.

She took off her helmet, then removed her leather vest. Despite the passing traffic, she removed her shirt, leaving her in nothing but a sports bra. Without paying any attention to the honks she was getting from the passing cars, she put her vest back on. Then she wound her hair back under her helmet, jammed it on her head and swung her leg over the seat of the bike.

The engine beneath her roared to life, then settled into a throaty rumble as she took off.

Less than a mile down the highway, a deer came bounding out of the trees at the side of the road. Sonora had to swerve to keep from hitting it. This time, when she got the Harley under control, she began to look for a safe place to cross.

She might be hardheaded, but she wasn't stupid. For whatever reason, she'd gone too far east. She thought of the exit she'd just passed, and the odd feeling that had come over her as she'd read the words.

Indian Nation Turnpike.

For the same reason that had taken her this far east, she felt she was now supposed to go south. She waited until there was a break in the traffic, and rode across the eastbound lanes and into the wide stretch of grass in the center median. She paused there, until she caught an opening in the westbound lanes and accelerated.

It didn't take her long to find the southbound exit to the Indian Nation Turnpike, and when she took it, it felt right. Pausing at the stop sign at the end of the exit ramp, she took a deep breath and then accelerated.

The moment she did, it felt as if the wheels on the Harley had turned to wings. The wind cooled her body and she felt lighter than air.

Adam loaded the last sack of groceries into the seat of his pickup truck and then slid behind the wheel. As soon as he turned it on, he noticed his fuel gauge registered low. He lived too far up into the mountains to risk running out of gas, so he backed up and drove to the gas station at the end of the street.

As he pumped the gas, a sweat bee zipped past his nose, then took a second run back at his arm. He took out his handkerchief and wiped the sweat from his brow. As he did, he heard the deep, throaty growl of a motorcycle engine and, out of nothing but curiosity, turned and found himself staring into the simmering fires of a setting sun.

For a moment, he was blinded by the glare, unable to see the rider or the bike. Quickly, he looked away, then shaded his face and looked again.

Breath caught at the back of his throat.

The bike and the rider were silhouetted against the heat and the sun as it paused on the horizon of an ending day. Despite the heat, Adam shivered. Although he knew it was an optical illusion, both rider and bike appeared to be on fire.

He was still staring when the illusion faded and the rider wheeled the bike into the empty space beside Adam's truck. He heard the pump kick off, signaling that his tank was full, and still he couldn't bring himself to move.

He didn't know when he realized that the rider was a woman, but he knew the moment she took off her helmet and turned to face him, that he'd been waiting for her all of his life.

When their gazes connected, she gasped, then staggered

backward. If Adam hadn't reacted so swiftly, she would have fallen over her bike. And the moment he touched her, he flinched as if he'd been burned.

"You came," he said softly.

Sonora looked down at his fingers that were curled around her bare arms. She could feel him. She could see him. But that had happened before. The test would now be if she could move.

She took a step back. To her surprise, her feet moved. In a panic, she wrenched away from his grasp.

"I'm awake," she muttered, more to herself than to him. She rubbed her arms where he'd been holding her, then looked up.

"Do you see me?"

He looked at her face as if trying to imprint every line and curve into his mind forever. There was no mistaking who she was, or why she was here. But from the little bit she'd just said, he suspected she was not in on the deal.

"Yes, I see you," he said softly.

Sonora exhaled a shaky breath. She didn't know what to say next.

"Do you know why you're here?" he asked.

She shook her head.

"And yet you came?" he asked.

She thought of the nights and days of hallucinations and was halfway convinced that this was nothing but a repeat of the same.

"It seemed I had no choice," she muttered.

"Your father waits for you," he said.

Sonora jerked as if he'd just slapped her. She was disgusted with herself for being so gullible. Whatever had been happening to her, now she knew it was a dream.

"I don't have a father," she said angrily.

"But you do," Adam said. "Have you ever heard your mother mention a man by the name of Franklin Blue Cat?"

She snorted in a very unlady-like manner, and added a succinct curse word to boot.

"Mother? I don't have one of those either," she said. "I was dumped on the doorstep of a Texas orphanage. The details of the ensuing years are hardly worth repeating. And now that this little mystery is over with, I'm out of here."

Adam winced. Franklin would be devastated by this news, and he couldn't let her leave. Not until they'd met face to face.

"You've come all this way. Don't you at least want to talk to him?"

"Why? He never bothered to look me up."

Adam heard old anger in her voice. The story wasn't his to explain, but if he didn't convince her of something, she would be gone before Franklin got a chance to state his case.

"Franklin didn't know about you. He still doesn't."

Sonora shook her head. "You're not making sense. And by the way, who the hell are you?"

"Adam Two Eagles."

She tried not to stare, but it was surreal to be standing here having this conversation with a specter from her dreams.

"So, Mr. Two Eagles…what do you do for a living…besides haunt people's dreams?"

Adam stifled a gasp of surprise. He'd been in her dreams? This, he hadn't known. The Old Ones had really done a job on her.

"I haunt nothing," he said quietly. "I used to be in the army. Now I'm a healer for my people, the Kiowa. I know you're Franklin's daughter, but I don't know your name or what you do."

"Sonora Jordan is my name. I'm an agent with the DEA." Then she turned the focus back on him. "So…Adam Two Eagles. You call yourself a healer."

He nodded once.

She reached behind her, felt the seat of her Harley, and clung to it as the only recognizable thing on which she could focus.

"Healer…as in medicine man or shaman, or whatever it is you people call your style of voodoo?" she asked.

"Healer, as in healer," he said. "And my people are your people, too. Whether you accept it or not, you are half Kiowa."

The words hit Sonora where it hurt—deep in the old memories of childhood taunts about being a throw-away child with no family and no name. She'd lived her entire life branded by two words that a priest and a nun had chosen out of thin air and given to the latest addition to their orphanage. Sonora because it was the priest's home town, and Jordan for no reason that she knew other than that they felt by not giving her a Latino name, she might have a better chance at a decent life. A quixotic thought for two devout Catholics who believed that everyone was equal in the eyes of God.

"You can't prove that," she muttered.

"Well…actually, I can," he said. "You've come all this way. You don't have to believe me. Follow me if you dare, and see for yourself."

Sonora thought of the handgun tucked into the storage behind the seat and then of how far she'd let herself be guided by a whim. What could it hurt? If she had to, she could take him. Besides, maybe this would finally put an end to being a walking nightmare just waiting to happen.

Adam watched her eyes, only guessing at the jumble of thoughts that must be going through her head.

"I won't hurt you," he added.

She fixed her gaze on his face, remembered the last thing he'd said to her in her dream, and then sighed. "I know that," she said.

Her assurance was startling.

"Why do you say that with such confidence?" Adam asked.

"I'm here because I fell into some sort of twilight zone. I'm here because I keep dreaming of a man who's either sick or dying. And I'm here because you keep haunting my dreams."

Again, she mentioned seeing him in her dreams. Intrigued, he had to ask. "What am I doing in your dreams?"

"Trying to seduce me…I think."

He wondered if he looked as startled as he felt.

"Indeed," he drawled. "And did I succeed?"

Thunder rumbled in the distance.

Sonora glanced up at the sky. Either she holed up in another motel until this storm passed, or she followed this man. Despite the fact that she'd seen his face in her dreams, she didn't know him. For all she knew, he might try to harm her. Then she sighed. Miguel Garcia wanted her dead. So what was new? It was either the devil she knew, or the one she didn't.

"I have one question to ask you," she said, ignoring the fact that she had not answered his.

He shrugged. "Then ask."

"This man you claim to be my father. Does he have a wind chime on his front porch that looks like a dreamcatcher?"

Despite the depth of his tribal beliefs, Adam was taken aback by the question.

"Yes."

"And does he have a hobby of carving things out of wood?"

Adam thought of his friend's fame that was known all over the world by those who indulged in his particular brand of art.

"Yes, you could say that," he said.

"And…a few days ago, was he taken ill?"

Now Adam was feeling out of kilter.

"You have seen all of this…in dreams?"

She shrugged, then nodded.

"The Old Ones have been playing with you," he said softly.

"Who?"

"Never mind," he said. "If you want to meet your father, then follow me."

"I need gas."

"I will wait."

She reached for the nozzle to the pump, quickly filled the tank, and then dashed into the station to pay.

Adam saw Franklin in every movement she made, from the cut of her features, to the way she moved when she walked—with her toes pointed inward just the tiniest bit and with the grace of a young filly at one with the world. She was a woman with copper-colored skin and long legs that life had saddled with a hefty portion of defiance. She and Franklin would get along just fine.

When she came out and mounted her bike, Adam was already rolling out of the station and onto the street.

She stuffed her hair back beneath her helmet, then fired up the engine. She was on Adam Two Eagles's tail before he passed the city limits sign.

Chapter 6

Sonora was still trying to wrap her mind around the fact that, not only was the man she'd dreamed of actually real, but that she was following him up a mountain without knowing where she was going. It was against every safeguard she'd been taught, and against every instinct she had. And yet she was doing it.

It was the first time in her life that she'd questioned the wisdom of having no personal ties. Before, it had been not only convenient, but wise. Without family, bad guys had no leverage against agents like her. But she'd never been faced with this particular situation. She wanted someone to know where she was and what she was doing, if for no other reason than to have a place to start looking for her, should she suddenly disappear.

Even as she was thinking the thoughts, something told her she was overstating the obvious. Adam Two Eagles had made no threats toward her. She didn't feel uneasy around him and she was a good judge of character. She wasn't afraid of Adam Two Eagles, but she was uncomfortable with what he represented.

Frustrated by thoughts that just kept going in circles, she began to focus on the beauty of the mountain, instead. Pine and cedar trees grew in great abundance, as well as knobby-barked Black Jack trees—a cousin of the oak. Every so often she would see a bird fly out from among the branches of a tree, and then disappear into another.

She thought of what it would be like to live up here, so far away from the conveniences of city living. One would have to be very secure to live so alone. Then it occurred to her that she lived in a city among thousands and was as alone as anyone could be. It was an eye-opening realization to know that it wasn't where you lived, but how you lived, that made lonely people.

Obviously, Franklin Blue Cat was alone, but if he was as secure within himself as Adam, she doubted that he was very lonely.

Just when she thought they would never arrive at their destination, Adam began to slow down, then came to a complete stop.

Sonora was forced to stop daydreaming and focus on the immediate. Up to now, the road had been blacktop, but she saw that, at the fork, the road became dirt. She realized she was about to eat dust.

When Adam leaned his head out of the window and waved her over, it became apparent he was concerned with the same thing.

"If you follow me too closely, you will be covered in dust."

She flipped up the visor on the helmet so that she could more easily be heard. "I'll manage," she said.

"Still, if you want to lay back a little, I thought I'd tell you where we're going so that you don't miss a turn."

Sonora thought about it and decided that a serial killer probably wouldn't give her a chance to get away like this. His offer went a long way toward easing her already suspicious mind.

"Yeah, okay, I see your point," she said.

"Good," Adam said, then pointed to the left. "Four miles down this way, you'll come to another fork in the road. Take the right fork, which goes up the mountain, and follow it. Franklin's home is at the end of the road. You'll see a couple of signs along the way that say Blue Cat Sculptures."

Sonora frowned. "Really? Does he sell arts and crafts from his home, or something?"

"No." Then he grinned. "I think there are a few more surprises in store for you. Your father is world renowned for his carvings."

"The bird," Sonora muttered.

Adam frowned. "I'm sorry, what did you say?" he asked.

"Oh, nothing," she said. "Let's go. I need to get this over with. I don't want to have to find my way off this mountain in the dark."

Adam's frown deepened. "There is no need for that to happen," he said. "Your father will welcome you."

"How could he when he didn't know I existed?"

Adam eyed the woman, accepting her defensiveness as understandable, yet wondering how much of the spiritual world of the Kiowa she would be able to accept.

"It is your father's story to tell," Adam said. "So, are you ready?"

"As I'll ever be," she muttered, and waited for him to drive away. As soon as he'd gone about a half mile down the road, she revved up the engine and followed.

* * *

Franklin was sitting on the porch when he heard the sound of a car coming up the road. It wasn't out of the ordinary for people to come unannounced, but he wasn't in the mood to cater to strangers. Still, his good manners bade him to deal with it, just as he was dealing with the leukemia ravaging his body.

When the truck appeared at the curve in the road, he breathed a sign of relief. It was Adam. He was always welcome.

Franklin stood, then lifted his arm in a greeting as Adam pulled up to the yard and stopped. He was part way off the steps when he realized that someone had been following Adam's truck.

Stifling a frown, he took a deep breath and put on his game face. When he saw that it was a rider on a motorcycle, he paused politely.

"Adam, it's good to see you," Franklin said, and then pointed down the road with his chin. "He with you?"

Adam stifled a smile, and then nodded.

Franklin sighed. "This has not been a good day."

Adam put a hand on his old friend's arm. "I'm sorry to hear that, old friend, but I have good news. That's about to change."

Franklin flinched. The eagle had warned him a change was coming. Was it already here?

The rider pulled up beside Adam's truck and then parked. It was when he started to dismount that Franklin realized the he was a she. Even in black leather, the body was definitely feminine.

He glanced at Adam, but Adam only smiled at him, then shrugged, as if to say, wait and see. Franklin sighed. These days, he was not so good at waiting for anything.

The rider leaned slightly forward as she took off the helmet, and as she lifted her head, a long, black sweep of hair fanned out, then fell loosely down the back of her neck. Even though she had yet to face him, Franklin felt an odd sense of familiarity.

"Adam?"

"Just wait," Adam said.

In that moment, Sonora Jordan turned, and for the second time today, found herself face to face with the other man from her dreams.

"This is too weird," she muttered, and refused to let herself be overwhelmed by the fact that this man claimed he was her father.

Franklin was shaking. He couldn't quit staring at her face.

"Who are you?" he asked.

Sonora looked at Adam, then frowned. "I thought you said he knew I was coming."

Adam decided it was time for him to intervene. "Franklin, the Old Ones have delivered what you asked for. This is Sonora Jordan. She's an agent with the DEA."

Sonora frowned. "What Old Ones? What are you talking about?" She backed up and laid her hand on the storage compartment behind the seat of the Harley. It made her feel safer to be close to the gun. "Is this some trick Garcia has pulled to get me alone, because I warn you, if it is, I won't—"

"No. No," Franklin whispered. "It's no trick. It's a miracle. I asked Adam to find my child. And you have come."

Sonora looked at Adam. "I don't get it. You didn't find me. I found you."

"Actually, it was neither," Adam said. "The Old Ones found you. They are the ones who have guided your path. They are the ones who have brought you to this place."

"What are you talking about? Who are these Old Ones you keep talking about?"

Franklin waved her question away as he took her by the hand.

"Forgive me, but I just had to touch you. You are so beautiful. My heart is full of joy."

"Look," Sonora said. "I appreciate your kindness, but how can you be certain that—"

"Come into my house. I'll prove it to you," Franklin said, and then turned and strode to the porch and up the steps without waiting to see if she was behind him.

Sonora glared at Adam. "I'm not falling for all this ghost and spirit crap."

"Suit yourself," he said. "But consider this…how else did you come to be in this place?"

She flashed on the hallucinations and dreams she'd been having and glared even harder.

"My boss told me to get lost for a while. That's how. I've got one man already on my back, trying to kill me. So, if you're in mind of doing anything similar, you need to get in line."

Adam froze. His voice deepened as his eyes went cold. "You are in danger?"

"Oh Lord…I don't know…yes, probably. At least enough that my boss told me to leave Phoenix."

"Come, come," Franklin called from the doorway. "You must see to believe."

Sonora gave Adam one last warning glance. "Just don't mess with me, okay?"

Adam didn't answer.

Sonora exhaled angrily, took her gun out of the compartment and put it in the back waistband of her pants, beneath her leather vest, then stomped into the house.

"So what do you have to show me?" Sonora said.

Franklin handed her a photo that he'd taken from the mantel over the fireplace.

Sonora eyed it casually, then stifled a gasp.

"Who is she?" she asked, pointing at the woman in the photo.

"My mother, and he is my father. It was taken on their wedding day."

"Good Lord," Sonora whispered, then carried it to a table in the hall and the mirror that hung above it.

She kept looking from the photo to her face and then back again until Adam took it from her hands and held it up beside her. Were it not for old-fashioned hair and clothing, and the man in the picture, she would have sworn the picture was of her.

"I look like her," Sonora said, and then bit her lip to keep from weeping. In all of her twenty-nine years, she'd never had the luxury of saying that before.

Franklin walked up behind her. Adam stepped back. Now Sonora was seeing herself, and Franklin Blue Cat, and seeing the similarities in their features. Her emotions were out of control. They went from jubilation, knowing she'd found a family, to hurt and anger that he'd never come looking for her. She wanted to cry, and settled for anger.

"Why?" she muttered.

"Why, what?" Franklin asked.

"Why am I just learning you existed?"

Franklin took her by the hand. "Please, may we sit down? I'm not feeling very well."

"What's wrong?" she asked as he led her to a sofa.

Franklin shrugged. "I have leukemia and the medicines have quit working. I am dying."

Sonora reeled from the news. She'd known he wasn't

well, and had even had the thought that he was dying, but to hear her suspicions were actually true made her sick to her stomach. This wasn't fair. She'd spent her entire life alone. Why would she be reunited with her only living family only to have him snatched away? How cruel was this?

"I'm so sorry," she mumbled, and bit her lip to keep from wailing.

Franklin nodded. "Such is life," he said, then brushed the topic aside. "Did your mother ever mention my name?"

Sonora smiled bitterly. "My mother, as you put it, dumped me on the doorstep of a Texas orphanage when I was less than a day old. I was named by a priest and a nun and dumped in a baby bed with two other babies. My earliest memory is of sitting in the corner of the bed and bawling because one of the bigger kids had taken my bottle and drank my milk."

Franklin reeled as if he'd been slapped. "You're not serious?"

She laughed to keep from crying. "Oh, but I am. She didn't want me and that's okay. I can take care of myself."

Franklin shook his head as tears unashamedly ran down his face. When she would have moved away, he took her hands, then held them fast against his chest.

"No. No. That is never okay. I am sorrier than I can tell you, but it's not okay. I didn't know until a few weeks ago that you might even exist. That's when I asked Adam for help."

Sonora shook her head. "That's what I still don't get. How did you come to believe you had a child? Who told you?"

"I had a dream," he said. "I have it often. It's always of your mother, whom I loved more than life. It's a repeat of our last day together, and how sad I am that she's moving away, even though I begged her to stay. Only this time the dream was different and it made me believe that your mother's spirit was trying to tell me to search for you."

"You're serious."

"Very."

Sonora pointed to Adam. "So, where does he come in?"

"He's the healer for our tribe. I am full-blood Kiowa. I have no brothers or sisters, and after your mother left, I never had another woman. I am the last of my people…or at least I was…until Adam sent for you."

"Both of you keep saying that, but I don't understand. How did he send for me when he didn't even know if I existed?"

"I made medicine," Adam said. "I told the Old Ones what Franklin wanted. They are the ones who looked for you. They are the ones who found you. They are the ones who have given you your dreams that led you to us."

"Oh…oh, whatever," Sonora muttered. "I can't deal with all that hocus pocus right now."

"It doesn't matter," Franklin said. "All that matters is that you are here."

Outside, there was a quick flash of lightning.

"It is going to rain. Will you stay?" Franklin asked. "I have many rooms in this house and yet I live in it all alone. I would welcome your company for as long as you can be here."

She thought about the danger her presence might cause, and then decided there was no way on earth that Miguel Garcia would ever find her here. Besides, she wasn't just curious, she ached to know this man who was claiming her. She wanted to know everything there was to know about the people whose blood ran through her veins.

"Yes, I'll stay, and thank you," she said. "I'll just go get my bag off the Harley."

"I'll get it," Adam said, "but then I must be going. I have animals to feed before dark."

He hurried outside, untied the bag from the back of the Harley and carried it into the house where Franklin was waiting.

"How can I ever thank you?" Franklin said, and then threw his arms around Adam and hugged him fiercely.

"It's the Old Ones you must thank," Adam said, then added, "Call if you need me."

Sonora was standing behind an easy chair, watching the two men part company. She felt like the outsider she really was, and had a sudden urge to jump on her bike and leave before she became too involved to let go. Then Adam turned his attention to her.

"Franklin has my number. Call me if you need me."

She made no comment, unwilling to admit that she didn't want him to leave.

Adam refrained from looking at her again. It was difficult enough not to let what he was thinking show through. Somehow, he didn't think Franklin would thank him for lusting after his newfound daughter.

"Come tomorrow," Franklin said. "I'll make breakfast."

Adam arched an eyebrow. Franklin's fry bread was famous on the mountain.

"Fry bread, too?"

Franklin smiled. "Sure."

"What's fry bread?" Sonora asked.

Both men looked at her and then shook their heads.

"It won't look good if word gets out that Franklin Blue Cat's daughter has never had fry bread," Adam said.

Franklin smiled. "You are right," he said. "So…my first duty as a father will be to introduce her to it."

Sonora caught herself smiling back. "Am I being the butt of a big joke?"

"Oh no," they said in unison. Then Adam added. "Your father often makes fry bread at the stomp dances."

"Stomp dances?"

They looked at her and then smiled again.

"You have a lot to learn about your people," Franklin said, then his smile went sideways. "I will teach you what I can with the time I have left."

Sonora nodded, then looked away. "Maybe you could tell me where you want me to sleep. I would like to wash off some of the dust before we talk any more."

"I'll be going now," Adam said. "See you for breakfast."

Sonora picked up her bag as Franklin led the way down a hall.

"These rooms are cool and catch plenty of breeze. However, there is an air conditioning unit if you wish to be cooler. The medicine I take makes me cold, so I don't often use the main one in the house any more."

"This is beautiful," Sonora said, overwhelmed by the subdued elegance. There were royal blue sheers at the windows, as well as vertical blinds. A matching blue and gold tapestry covered a king-size bed and there was a large Navajo rug on the floor in front of it. But it was the carving of a small kitten that caught her eye. It was lying on its back with its feet up in the air, batting at a dragonfly that had landed on its nose.

She moved toward it, touched it lightly, then picked it up. "I can't believe this is wood. It looks real."

Franklin smiled. It was praise of the highest kind. "Thank you. It would honor me if you would accept it as a gift."

Sonora's eyes widened. "Oh. I didn't mean to suggest…I couldn't possibly…"

Franklin put a hand on her shoulder. "Please. You're my daughter. Of course you must have this."

Sonora ran a thumb along one of the paws, tracing each tiny cut that gave the appearance of fine hair.

"This is magnificent," she whispered.

"I call the piece, Friends," Franklin said.

"It's perfect," Sonora said, and then held it close as she looked up into his face—a face so like her own. "Today has been overwhelming," she said. "There is so much I don't understand—so much I don't know how to explain. I've never had family of my own, so if I do something wrong, I beg your forgiveness ahead of time."

"You can do no wrong," Franklin said. "You're the one who's been wronged. I don't understand how this happened, but if I'd known about you, I would have moved heaven and earth to bring you home."

Threatened by overwhelming emotions, Sonora shuddered. "If this is a dream, I don't want to wake up."

Franklin shook his head. "It is no dream. Now, I have one request to ask of you."

"If I can. What do you need?"

"To hold my daughter."

Sonora hesitated long enough to put down the sculpture, then turned and walked into his arms.

Franklin stifled a sob as she laid her cheek against his chest. For the first time since he'd received the news of his death sentence, he was angry all over again. This wasn't fair. Why should they be reunited like this, only to know it would soon come to an end?

It was almost dark by the time Adam got home. He finished his chores in the dark and then hurried inside, reaching shelter only moments before the heavens turned loose of the rain.

Wind blew. Thunder rumbled. Lightning flashed.

He ate a lonely meal and thought of the breakfast tomorrow, knowing that, for a short time, he would be with Sonora again.

He didn't know what was going to happen between them, but he didn't want the relationship to end before they had a chance to know one another.

He thought of Franklin, wondering how he was going to take finding a daughter and losing his life.

Rain blew against the kitchen window as he washed the dishes from his evening meal. Lightning flashed, momentarily revealing the wildly thrashing trees and limbs and the flow of rainfall funneling through the yard to the creek below his house.

Then another, more sinister thought reared its head.

Sonora had said she was in danger.

He feared she was understating the issue. The soldier in him wanted to take her to a place of safety and guard her against the world. But the healer in him knew there was another way.

His eyes narrowed as he dried his hands and moved from the kitchen, to the medicine room.

He paused in the doorway, thinking of a stranger on Sonora's trail, and then moved with purpose to the shelves. Without hesitation, he chose the items he needed, then carried them outside onto the porch. Sheltered from the rain, he lit a swatch of dried sweetgrass, then purified the air with the smoke.

He fell into the old language as easily as he breathed, turned to the north and began to chant, telling the Old Ones of the danger to one of their own, beseeching them to protect her when he could not. Then he repeated the request to the east, then the south, and finally the west.

A wild crack of lightning hit the ground only yards

away from his house. Adam staggered backward from the force of the strike. The scent of sulfur was heavy in the air. As he stood, the wind suddenly changed and blew rain up under the eaves of the porch and into Adam's face.

He took it as a sign that they'd heard.

It was done.

Chapter 7

Sonora spent the rest of the evening in a daze. It was difficult to wrap her mind around the fact that she not only had a father, but that she was actually in his house. While the premise was far-fetched and almost too good to be true, whatever doubts she might have had about being his daughter ended the moment she'd seen her grandmother's picture.

Thinking about how she got here could make her crazy if she dwelled on it, so she didn't. For a woman who'd spent all of her adult life dealing in truth and facts, accepting the notion of being guided by what amounted to ghosts seemed ridiculous. Still, however it had happened, she was grateful to be here.

And, Franklin, who was normally shy and reticent toward strangers, was struggling to give her space. The last thing he wanted was to scare her off, but he felt a constant need to be with her. With his life span already limited, he was resentful that their time together was destined to be short.

So, while they wrestled to find comfort with each other, the thunderstorm that threatened earlier had come full force. Sonora and Franklin ate their evening meal with an accompaniment of thunder and lightning, then washed dishes with rain splattering against the windows. After that, Franklin had taken her on a tour of the house, only to have it interrupted by a power failure. Sonora had embarrassed herself by panicking when the lights had gone out. By the time Franklin found flashlights and lit a few candles, the power was on.

Now they sat in front of a television without paying any attention to the programming, trying to find points of connection between their separate lives.

Sonora was fascinated with his artistic skills and was going through a photo album that represented a complete set of his work once he'd turned a hobby into a profession. She was in awe of where he'd been, and the heads of states he'd met in faraway countries.

Franklin, on the other hand, was trying to hide his dismay at the profession his only child had chosen.

"So, when did you begin working with the DEA?" he asked.

Sonora turned a page in the album, then looked up.

"It seems like forever, but I guess it's been about seven or eight years now. I had just turned twenty-one. I'm twenty-nine now. I'll be thirty in September."

Franklin's nostrils flared. It was the only indication he gave of realizing there was another slot to be filled.

"Your birthday," he said softly.

Sonora nodded, then stopped.

"Oh. Yes. Another gap in our knowledge of each other,

which I can quickly fix. My birthday is September 12. I'm five-feet-ten inches tall in my bare feet. I wear a size ten in clothes, and I love chocolate."

He tried to smile and hugged her, thankful that she was trying to make light of the vast gap between them, because the truth of it broke his heart.

"You are tall, like me," he said. "Your mother, Leila, was a small woman, but she had a big laugh." His smile faded. "It was the first thing I loved about her." Then he shook his head. "But that's for another time. I was born on June 4th in a storm cellar while a tornado blew away the house that was here. This is the one they built to replace it, so it is the only home I've ever known."

Sonora nodded, as she listened to him talk, but she wasn't listening as intently as she should have been. Instead, she was marking the way his left eyebrow arched as he told something funny—noticing his slim hands and long fingers; hands of an artist. His skin was darker than hers, but not by much, and she suspected part of the washed-out color of his skin was due to his illness. She thought of seeing him unconscious on the floor and not knowing the connection between them, and how blessed she was to be sitting here now.

Then she thought of Adam coming to his rescue.

"Tell me about Adam Two Eagles," she said.

Franklin had sensed what seemed to be interest between the two and could only hope something came of it.

"His father was my best friend," he said. "His mother was a distant cousin on my mother's side."

"We're related?" she asked, unaware that she was frowning.

This time, Franklin allowed himself a grin. "Only in the most distant sense of the word. Probably what would amount to a sixth or seventh cousin."

"Oh. Well. That hardly counts, does it?"

Franklin's grin spread. "Definitely does not count."

Sonora realized he was having fun at her expense, and made a face at him. "It's not what you think. I was asking only because I would want to know of any relatives."

Franklin sighed, and then took her hand in his. "I'm afraid, when it comes to close family, we're it." Then Franklin shifted gears to Sonora's life. "Have you ever been married?"

"No." She thought of Buddy and smiled. "Not even close, although I've had a couple of relationships and gotten a good friend from one of them."

"Friends are good," Franklin said.

Sonora thought of the dream she'd had of Adam, of the whisper of his breath on the back of her neck, and the challenge he'd given her right before she'd awakened.

"Come to me," he'd said.

And she would have done it—willingly. However, faced with the real man and not one out of some dream, she was far more discerning. As intriguing as he was—as handsome and compelling as he was—he was still a stranger.

Unaware of the places her mind had taken her, Franklin had shifted a few mental gears of his own.

"In the morning, I'll show you the boundaries of our land," Franklin said.

Sonora was so taken aback by the fact that he'd referred to the property as "ours" that she could hardly speak. Still, she felt a need to slow him down from committing to things he might later come to regret.

"Franklin…wait. Please. You don't need to do this," she said.

"Do what?" Franklin asked.

"Include me in your life so quickly. It's not 'our' land, it's yours."

Franklin frowned, then shook his head.

"That's where you're wrong," he said. "Everything I do these days is done quickly. I don't have the luxury of assuming there will be a tomorrow. And, knowing you exist and that you are of my flesh is a joy you don't understand. To the Native American, family is everything, and my family has lived in this area for generations. The last four generations are buried here, and until your arrival, that heritage was going to end with my death. Now, I can die with peace. Even if you choose not to live here, it will always be yours, and hopefully, the generations that come after."

Sonora was too moved to speak. All she managed to do was nod and then look away.

Franklin sighed. "I did not mean to upset you, but these are things you must know."

Sonora's voice was shaking, but she looked him square in the eyes. "And, by the same token, you cannot know what this means to me. I have lived twenty-nine years without belonging anywhere or to anyone. Now, to have been given both at the same time is almost more than I can comprehend. I'm not upset. I'm overwhelmed."

Franklin relaxed, then patted her hand. "Then this is good, yes?"

Sonora sighed. "Yes, this is good."

"So…would you mind very much if, from time to time, I called you daughter?"

Sonora blinked away tears. "I would be honored. And for the same reasons, it would be wonderful to know I could call you Dad."

There was a time in Franklin's life when he would have hesitated to let someone see him cry, but that time had long since passed. His eyes filled with tears as he took her in his arms and held her.

They might have stayed there longer, but Sonora felt his body trembling and knew it was from fatigue. Without calling attention to his weakness, she claimed exhaustion on her own.

"I hate to be the party-pooper, but this has been a long day. If you don't mind, I think I'd like to go to bed."

"Of course," Franklin said, and got up as she stood.

"So...you invited Adam for breakfast, didn't you?" Franklin grinned.

"Quit that," she muttered. "I'm just asking so I won't over-sleep. That would be rude."

"Oh, definitely, that would be rude," Franklin said, and then they both laughed out loud. "He'll probably show up around nine. He knows I don't get up as early as I used to."

"I'm a pretty good cook," Sonora said. "If you show me where stuff is, I'd loved to make the meal."

Franklin took a slow breath, and then touched her face with the back of his hand. "And I would love to eat your cooking," he said, then puffed out his chest in an exaggerated manner. "My daughter cooks for me tomorrow. If someone had told me I would be saying these words tonight, I would have called them crazy."

"So it's a deal?" Sonora asked, and held out her hand.

Franklin shook it. "It's a deal," he said.

Sonora nodded and started to leave the room, then she paused and looked back.

Franklin was watching her go.

She bit her lip, then took a slow breath. Revealing her vulnerability was more difficult than she'd imagined it would be. Still, she'd waited a lifetime to say these words and she wasn't going to cheat herself out of the opportunity because she was afraid.

"Night...Dad."

Franklin smiled.

"Goodnight…daughter. Sleep well."

Soon, the house went dark and both father and daughter slept with a peace in their hearts they'd never known before.

Adam, on the other hand, didn't get much sleep. His dreams were troubled with a faceless enemy stalking Franklin's daughter. Finally, he woke up in a sweat, and abandoned his bed for the swing on his front porch.

The air was cooler and rain-washed. Bullfrogs sang from the overflowing creek while their tinier cousins, the tree frogs contributed to the chorus. The quarter moon hung low in the sky, shyly showing its face from behind the swiftly moving clouds.

Adam walked to the edge of the steps and then looked up, inhaling deeply as he combed his fingers through his hair.

There was a power in the dark that daylight didn't share. He'd known it since childhood, and it had saved his life more than once during his years with the military. Night was a shield for those who needed it, and kept secrets better than a best friend ever could. It protected, and at the same time, left the weak more vulnerable.

Adam thought about the creek running out its banks down the hill below. If it wasn't for the copperheads between him and the water, he'd chance a midnight dip. However, his foolish days were long gone, and he would gladly settle for a cold shower.

He was about to go back inside when he heard a coyote yip. Within seconds, another answered, and then another and another, until the night was alive with their calls. He smiled. It was one of the sounds of the Kiamichi Mountains that he loved most.

He thought of the years he'd spent in foreign countries, living his life for the American government instead of for himself, and said a quiet prayer of thanks that he'd lived to make it home.

He stood on the porch and gave the coyotes their due by waiting until the chorus had ended.

"Good job, boys," he said softly, then started into the house. He was crossing the threshold when his cat, Charlie, slipped between his legs and darted beneath a chair.

He closed the door, then got down on his hands and knees and grinned at the cat who was peering at him from beneath the small space.

"What's wrong, old man? Coyotes make you a little nervous?"

"Rowrrr."

"I feel your pain," Adam said.

"Rrrpp?"

"Yeah, sure…why not?" Adam said. "I don't have anyone else fighting you for the space."

Since he'd been given permission, Charlie abandoned the space beneath the chair for a spot at the foot of Adam's bed.

Both males were soon sound asleep, taking comfort in the knowledge that, for tonight, they were not alone.

Miguel Garcia was in Amarillo, Texas, pacing the room of his motel with his cell phone up to his ear. He'd trailed Sonora Jordan this far and then had lost her. At this point, he knew he needed help and had been trying to contact some of his men in Juarez. But, no matter who he called, he got no answer. That alone was enough to make him nervous.

And, if he'd known the truth, nervous would have been an understatement. He didn't know that there was already a big upheaval in his organization that had nothing to do

with Enrique and Juanito's absences. He didn't know that
Jorge was moving in on territory that had been under Garcia control for years. And, he didn't know that Jorge had
given the DEA the description and tag number of the car
Miguel was driving. Miguel thought he was the hunter, but
in truth, he was also the prey.

Gerald Mynton was beside himself with frustration.
Twice, he'd missed phone calls from Sonora. He didn't
know what she was trying to pull, dropping out of sight like
this without staying in touch.

Yes, he knew he'd told her to get lost. But he hadn't expected her to actually do it. As far as he knew, she was in
imminent danger and he had no way of warning her about
it. So, in order to offset the chance that they might miss
connecting again, he was having all of his calls, both personal and professional, forwarded to his cell phone. No
matter what time of day or night a call came in, he would
get it. With this small assurance set in place, Mynton finally gave up and went to bed. And while he wasn't a praying kind of man, he still said a prayer of safekeeping for
Sonora before he could fall asleep.

Sonora woke abruptly, and for a moment, couldn't remember where she was. Then her gaze fell on the carving
of the kitten and the dragonfly and breath caught in her
throat.

Home.

She was home.

She glanced at the clock, then her eyes widened. It was
already seven-thirty and Adam was coming for breakfast.
She flew out of bed and raced into the bathroom. It was
the quickest shower she'd ever had. She dressed in a pair

of old jeans and a red, sleeveless T-shirt, and as an after-thought, pocketed her cell phone. Then she pulled her hair up on top of her head, securing it with an elastic band. She started to put on her tennis shoes, then decided against it and left the room in bare feet.

As she started down the hall, she could hear Franklin moving around in his room, so she knew he was up, but she was going to do her own investigating into what was available in the kitchen, without bothering him.

Before she started looking in the fridge, she made a big pot of coffee, hoping that the men liked it strong. Soon, the enticing aroma of freshly brewing coffee filled the air as she began looking to see what was available to cook.

It was easy to spot the bacon and eggs, and she found half a loaf of bread and two kinds of jelly in the refrigerator, as well. A set of canisters on the cabinet revealed flour and sugar. After digging through the pantry, she found a partially used bag of self-rising flour, a can of vegetable shortening and a small bottle of sorghum molasses. She was in business.

She turned on the oven to preheat, laid her cell phone on the counter out of the way, then dug through the cabinets and drawers until she found the rest of what she needed. It wasn't long until the smell of baking bread was added to the aromas drifting through the house.

Sonora was frying bacon when she sensed she was no longer alone. She looked up. Franklin was standing in the doorway to the kitchen. She smiled.

"Good morning. How did you sleep?" she asked, as he moved toward her.

Franklin touched her shoulder in a gentle, hesitant manner, then kissed the side of her cheek.

Sonora leaned against him for a fraction of a second,

then made herself smile, when all she wanted to do was cry. This family stuff was harder than she would have thought.

"I slept well," Franklin said. "And you?"

"Like a baby," Sonora said. "How are you feeling?"

He shrugged. "Some mornings are better than others."

She eyed the food she was making. "Does this bother you…I mean, the smells of food cooking? I didn't think that you might not be—"

Franklin held up a hand to silence her. "It smells wonderful. I will drink some coffee and take my meds and maybe steal a piece of that bacon when it's done before Adam comes and eats all my food."

Sonora nodded and made herself smile, but she could tell he wasn't right. Either he was weak, or in pain, or possibly both. It broke her heart to think that she had just met this wonderful man and might lose him before they got to know each other the way father and daughter should.

She pretended not to notice his hand shaking as he poured coffee into a cup, and she busied herself making gravy when he counted out more than a dozen pills and swallowed them, one by one.

Biscuits had just come out of the oven when someone knocked on the front door.

Franklin looked up at the clock and grinned.

"Adam already? It's barely eight-thirty. I'm thinking he must really be hungry…or something."

Sonora heard the sarcasm in his voice and laughed in spite of herself. Franklin was obviously a big tease and she may as well face the fact that he wasn't going to give up alluding to Adam's interest in her.

"Probably smelled the biscuits," she said. "Want me to let him in?"

Franklin's smile widened. "Someone has to. Might as well be you."

She threw a pot holder at him.

Surprise lit his face as he caught it. This daughter of his had fire in her soul. But he should have known that. No one did what she did for a living without having a large amount of faith in herself. It made him sick at heart to think of her growing up so alone. It was a good thing that she'd had a strong belief in herself, because there had been no one else to do it for her.

He heard Adam's deep voice, then the sound of Sonora laughing. He smiled. It had been years since such joy had filled this house. His blessing was that he'd lived long enough to hear it.

"Good morning, Franklin," Adam said, as he followed Sonora into the kitchen. Then he eyed the stove and the pan of biscuits. "You outdid yourself this morning, didn't you?"

Franklin beamed. "I did nothing but oversleep. My daughter has cooked our food this morning."

Sonora bit her lip to keep it from trembling as she cracked eggs into the hot skillet. This was nothing short of a miracle and she was frying eggs in this kitchen as if it was no big deal.

"I like mine over easy," Adam said.

Sonora jumped. She hadn't known he'd come up behind her.

"How many?" she asked.

"Two, please."

She grabbed another egg and broke it into the skillet beside the three that were already beginning to cook.

"What about you, Dad? How many eggs for you?"

"Oh…maybe one. My appetite isn't what it used to be."

Sonora turned around and frowned at Franklin. His

color was ashen, and there was a bead of sweat on his upper lip. She took a piece of bacon from the platter, handed it to him and pointed toward the table.

"Sit."

Franklin took the bacon and sat without argument. Adam looked startled by Sonora's perception, and without comment, poured himself a cup of coffee and sat down by Franklin.

Sonora noticed the way Adam cared for Franklin, subtly checking the older man's pulse, then shaking out two pain killers for him from a bottle in the cabinet. By the time the eggs were done, Franklin appeared to be feeling better.

Sonora carried the plates to the table, then added the biscuits, bacon and jelly. She poured up the gravy and refilled the coffee cups, then finally sat down.

Franklin eyed the table, then Adam, then Sonora.

"Today, I am truly blessed," he said softly. "And so I ask blessings for the food we are about to eat, and for the company of my daughter and my best friend."

"I am the one who's honored. Are those biscuits homemade?"

Sonora eyed Franklin, who appeared ready to offer another comment regarding her expertise in a kitchen, and headed him off.

"Yes, and before we get all carried away with praise for the cook, you should know that the eggs are getting cold," she said.

With that, she passed the biscuits down the table, trying not to appear too pleased when both men took two apiece to start with.

For a few minutes, little was said other than a request for something to be passed. It wasn't until Franklin was finishing his second biscuit that it occurred to him the food tasted good.

"Sonora, this food is very good," Franklin said. "Who taught you to cook like this?"

"Betty Crocker."

Adam grinned.

Franklin's eyebrow arched.

"THE Betty Crocker?"

"The one and only," Sonora added.

Adam snagged another biscuit, slathered it with butter and jelly, then toasted Sonora with it.

"Then…my compliments to the cook," he said.

But Franklin wasn't satisfied.

"You learned to cook like this from a book?"

Sonora shrugged.

"Pretty much. I got tired of eating out all the time, bought myself an old Betty Crocker cookbook from a library sale when I was…oh…probably eighteen or nineteen. After that, it was largely a case of trial and error. I did get a few pointers from an elderly woman who was my neighbor at the time."

Franklin lifted his head and then stared off into the distance. Sonora could tell that he was troubled, but she didn't understand.

"What's wrong? Are you feeling bad again? Maybe you should go lie down for a—"

"I'm sick, but not like you mean. I am sick at heart that you have marked every step in your life alone."

Sonora got up and put her arms around her father's neck and hugged him.

"You worry too much," she said. "I'm fine. I'm strong. And if you're feeling all that good, you can do dishes."

Franklin looked startled, then he laughed and pointed at Adam.

"Two Eagles will do the dishes."

Adam grinned. "It would be my pleasure. However, I hope you know that there's a house rule about the dishwasher getting to take home the leftovers."

Sonora frowned.

"There's nothing left but biscuits."

"Exactly," Adam said, and then grabbed the bread plate and headed for the cabinet.

"We will be outside on the back porch for a while," Franklin said. "When you've finished, please join us."

"Hmmpf? Oh…shurr," Adam mumbled.

Sonora wasn't sure, but she thought he'd just stuffed another biscuit in his mouth, then Franklin took her hand and led her outside.

"Let's sit here," he said, and pointed to a couple of wicker chairs at the north end of the porch.

They sat. Franklin took a deep breath, folded his hands in his lap, and then stared straight into Sonora's eyes.

"Now we ask questions of each other, and the answers must be honest."

Before they could start, Sonora heard the familiar ring of her cell phone that she'd left on the cabinet. At the same time, Adam called out.

"Sonora, your phone is ringing."

"The only person it could be is my boss," Sonora said. "I'd better get it."

Adam met her at the door and handed it to her as she came inside.

"Thanks," she said, glanced at the caller ID, then smiled. "I was right. It's my boss. This won't take a minute, okay?"

Franklin nodded, and then leaned back in the chair as Sonora answered.

"Hello."

Gerald Mynton breathed a huge sigh of relief.

"Thank God," he muttered. "You've been harder to find than the Loch Ness monster."

Sonora frowned. "What's wrong?"

Mynton sighed. There was no easy way to say this. "I'm afraid I have some bad news."

Sonora stilled. "How bad?"

"Your friend, Buddy Allen, is dead. We think Garcia got to him, trying to find you."

Sonora moaned. She didn't know it, but her face had gone white as a sheet.

"What happened to him?" she asked.

"It doesn't matter how. I don't know what this means, but before he died, Buddy said to tell you that 'he didn't tell'."

Sonora choked on a sob. Buddy the joker, the life of the party who could never shut up, yet he'd wanted her to know that he didn't tell Garcia anything about how she'd left town.

She took a deep breath and then made herself calm when all she wanted to do was start screaming. She compromised by shouting. "I asked you a question and I need an answer. What did Garcia do to him?"

Startled by her outburst, Franklin started to get up and go to her, but Adam beat him to it. Adam walked up behind her, put an arm around her waist, just to let her know she wasn't alone. To his surprise, her legs all but gave way.

"Easy, girl," Adam said softly. "We're here for you."

Sonora's knuckles were white from the grip she had on the phone and she was struggling to keep focused as she repeated herself one last time. "Please, Boss. I have to know."

Mynton was sick to his stomach to have to be the one to tell her. "He beat him, honey...bad. He beat him real bad."

She bent over and grabbed her stomach, certain that her breakfast was about to come up.

"Oh, God, oh God. It's my fault. I shouldn't have—"

"No, damn it. It's Miguel Garcia's fault," Mynton said. "And just so you know, he's on your trail."

Sonora straightened up with a jerk and cast a frantic glance at her father, and then at Adam. What evil had she brought to this beautiful place?

"How? How could he know where I am?" Sonora asked. "Nobody knew. Buddy sure as hell didn't. Even I didn't know where I was going and I'll bet my life I didn't leave a trail."

"Well, that's just it. You are betting your life and I don't like it. I want you to come in. We'll put you in protective custody and—"

"No. I will not hide from the bastard. Besides, how do you know he's following me?"

"He was last seen in Flagstaff. Did you go through there?"

Sonora shuddered.

"Yes, but so what? There are four different ways to leave that city."

"He's moving east."

"Shit."

Mynton heard her muffled curse.

"I'm sorry."

"Yeah," she said, swiping tears from her face even as she pulled herself out of Adam's arms. "I'm sorry, too, but not nearly as sorry as Garcia is going to be when I find him."

Mynton nearly dropped the phone. "What the hell do you mean...when you find him?"

"I'm not going to sit here like a Judas goat and let everyone else—"

Adam didn't know what was happening, but he could tell that it was bad. And, he could tell that Sonora was in trouble.

He grabbed her arm and mouthed the words, what's wrong?

She frowned, and waved him away.

He grabbed her arm again, and this time, said it out loud.

"What's wrong?"

Sonora rolled her eyes.

"Boss…hang on just a minute, okay?" Then she turned her pain into anger and lit into Adam. "It's business, Adam, my business, which means it's none of yours. I'm a big girl and I can take care of myself."

"Who's Buddy?"

Her face crumpled like a used napkin.

"My friend. He is…was…my friend. The man who wants me dead beat him to death, trying to find out where I was."

Franklin took the phone from Sonora's hands.

She was so surprised by his actions that she let him do it.

"Excuse me," Franklin said. "I'm Sonora's father, and whatever trouble she is in, we will help her deal with it."

Sonora grabbed the phone away. "Boss! It's me! Don't pay any attention to him. I'll be leaving here as soon as I can pack. I'm not going to have Garcia come looking for me here."

Mynton was too stunned to follow her conversation.

"I thought you were raised in an orphanage."

"I was, damn it, but—"

"Then how did you find your father?"

"It's a long story," she muttered.

"I don't know what's going on there," Mynton said. "But think a minute. No one knows you have family, so there's no one to look for. However, if you leave, how are you going to be sure that Garcia doesn't find them in his quest to look for you?"

"Because I'll find him first," she snapped.

"Yeah, well, Buddy Allen might have given you an argument with that thought."

Sonora reeled as if she'd been slapped.

"That's not fair," she mumbled, then swiped a shaky hand across her face. "I can't think right now. I'll call you later, okay?"

"Promise?" Mynton asked. "Oh. Wait. You're supposed to call a detective named Broyles with the Phoenix P.D. He's working Buddy's case."

"Yes, all right," she said, and then hung up.

For a moment, she stood with her head down and her shoulders shaking. Tears were rolling out of her eyes and down her face, but she wasn't making a sound.

Adam waited silently until he could take no more.

"You're not alone."

She put a hand over her eyes, and then turned away.

Franklin put a hand on her shoulder.

"You're not alone," he said, repeating Adam's words.

She lifted her head, looking first at her father, then at Adam. Whatever might have been between them was over before it began.

"I can't be here," she said softly. "I will bring death to this place if I stay."

Franklin waved his hand as if he was shooing a fly.

"Death is already here, Daughter. It's been here for months waiting for me to notice. Please, whatever is wrong, you must let us help you."

"It's DEA business," she muttered. "I can't get civilians involved in—"

Adam interrupted. "I spent twelve years with the army Rangers. I was good at what I did. You'll stay. We will help."

"It is settled," Franklin said.

Sonora was too overwhelmed to argue, and when they came to her and held her, she didn't say no.

Chapter 8

Once the shock of the call and the trauma of the morning had been dealt with, Franklin went inside to rest, leaving Adam and Sonora alone. Normally, she would have been defensive with a man she hardly knew, but she wasn't with Adam. She didn't bother with trying to figure out why. She just took his presence as the comfort she desperately needed, and finally let herself grieve.

Her eyes were shiny with unshed tears, and the sight hurt Adam's heart. As they walked beyond the yard into the shade of the forest, little by little, Adam drew out details of the relationship that had been between her and Buddy Allen. He wouldn't let himself think about the spurts of jealousy that came and went as he listened to her talking about a man with whom she'd once been intimate. He didn't want to admit, not even to himself, that he was envious of a dead man.

* * *

"So you dated Buddy for nine months. You must have some really good memories," Adam said gently.

Tears finally spilled over and rolled down her face as she paused beneath a large oak.

"You'd think so, wouldn't you? But all I can remember was constantly disappointing him. I was gone so much and he wanted more from the relationship than I was ever able to give."

"He wanted to marry you?" Adam asked.

"Something like that," Sonora said, then her voice broke. "And now he's dead…he's dead because of me. I told him my life was too complicated for commitments but he wouldn't listen." She choked on a sob and then covered her face with her hands. "Oh God, Adam, Garcia beat him to death. I can't get that out of my head."

Adam put his arms around her. Sonora stiffened. Accepting sympathy was as difficult for her to deal with as accepting advice. But he didn't turn her loose and she didn't pull away, and slowly, slowly, she began to relax. When that happened, the wall of her emotions crumbled. Before she knew it, she was sobbing.

"Yes, pretty lady…cry for your friend…and for yourself. Cry it all out," Adam whispered.

And she did.

A day passed, and then another, until an entire week had come and gone since Sonora's arrival. As per her father's wishes, she'd checked in every day with Mynton, just so she would stay up to date on the investigations. She'd called the Phoenix detective as she'd been asked to do, but had been unable to give him any information he didn't already have.

She knew that, after a possible sighting of Garcia in Amarillo, Wills and the task force had left Flagstaff to check it out, and upon arrival had gotten a positive ID. Problem was, by the time all of that had been confirmed, Garcia was long gone—destination unknown.

As for Miguel Garcia, it had taken big money and calling in some favors from an old friend of his father before he'd finally gotten some help. Now, four of the drug cartel's finest were combing the highways and the states bordering Texas and Oklahoma, trying to get a fix on the whereabouts of the missing DEA agent. Miguel had let it be known that it was worth a half million dollars to him to find Sonora Jordan.

While the men were searching, Garcia was forced to lay low. He now knew he had agents on his tail. He'd been assured by Emilio Rojas, the man who'd been his father's right hand, that not only did the DEA have agents on his trail, but they knew the make, model and tag number of the car he was driving. Once the significance of this news sank in, he felt sick. The only way that could have happened, was if he'd been betrayed.

Time and time again, he went over a mental list of people who'd helped get him across the border. There were any number who could have tipped off the DEA, but he kept remembering the man at the airport outside of Houston who'd brought him a car and money, and then so abruptly disappeared.

It stood to reason that this man could be the one who betrayed him. But then he would skip to the fact that Jorge Diaz had set everything up. Diaz was entirely responsible for successfully getting Miguel out of Mexico. He would have had access to the same information.

To go there in his mind, Miguel had to accept that Diaz would betray him, and he couldn't believe it, even though he had been unable to contact Diaz for days.

To be on the safe side, he'd sold his car at a used car dealer in Oklahoma City, bought a four-year old Jeep from a different car lot, driven thirty minutes East on I-40 to Shawnee, Oklahoma and had the Jeep painted black.

Before he left town, he'd stolen a Native American license plate from a member of the Muscogee Nation while the car was parked outside the Firelake Casino south of Shawnee. He'd driven off with no one the wiser, traveling as far as Tulsa, Oklahoma before going to ground.

There, he'd begun the business of disguising his appearance. He'd shaved his head and mustache, bought himself some western style clothes, including a pair of ostrich skin boots and a big black hat. By the time he added a large silver belt buckle to his wardrobe, his own mother would not have recognized him.

Feeling fairly safe about getting back out in the world, he thought about resuming his own search for Sonora, but decided to err on the side of caution. If his men didn't find her within the week, he was going to go back to Phoenix. Sonora Jordan couldn't stay gone forever, and he was a patient man.

Adam had not been to Franklin's house, or seen Sonora since the morning she'd received the news of her old friend's death. He relived their last moments together in his dreams—holding her close against his body—feeling the thrust of her breasts against his chest as she cried for another man. But in his dreams, her tears somehow turned to passion. They would lie down together beneath the sheltering limbs of the old oak. There would be whispers and promises and an ache so deep that it took Adam's breath away. What was driving him crazy was that, he kept waking up before they could make love. He was sick and tired of cold showers and aches that wouldn't go away.

She and Franklin didn't have a lot of time to play catch up, and he didn't want to intrude. But he wasn't a fool. He also didn't want to lose the small foothold he'd gained with her by staying gone too long. She was a stranger in every way that it mattered, and yet there was a part of him that knew he couldn't bear to let her go. He didn't know how much time she would give herself to stay on the mountain, but he wanted his share of it. The way he looked at it, he'd given them a week. His streak of generosity was over.

Franklin was having a bad day and, after breakfast, had gone back to bed. Sonora had quickly learned that, on these days, the best thing she could do for him was give him space and quiet. So when he went back to his room, she took his fishing pole and straw hat and headed for the pond at the back of the property.

She caught a few grasshoppers on the way and put them in a jar to use for bait just like Franklin had showed her. The wide brim on his old hat shaded her face while the sun had its way with the rest of her body. Even though it was hot, she knew she wouldn't burn. By the time she got to the pond, her T-shirt was stuck to the sweat on her back and she had some kind of weird-looking burrs in her socks. Still, she was happier than she could ever remember being.

On the second day of her arrival, Franklin had saddled up two of his horses and they'd ridden from one corner of the property to the other until she knew where Blue Cat land began and ended. It had given her a sense of identity that she'd never known.

So, today, as she baited her hook, she had the satisfaction of knowing that she was standing on Blue Cat land— about to fish in a Blue Cat pond.

She wrinkled her nose and asked an apology of the poor grasshopper that was still kicking on the hook as she tossed it in the water. The red and white bobber bounced a few times within the spreading ripples. After that, it was a case of sit and wait.

For Sonora, it was like living out a dream. As a child, she used to imagine the innocence of a life like this, with people who loved her sitting beside her. There would be a picnic and laughter and playing barefoot in the water. It wouldn't matter if anyone caught fish because they were together.

The sun was hot. Sonora's eyelids were drooping. The bobber was riding high in the still water like an empty ship, and she couldn't bring herself to care that she wasn't getting any nibbles.

Something tickled her arm. She brushed at it without looking. Then something tickled the back of her neck. She brushed at it as absently as she had her arm.

"If I was a bad guy, you'd be in trouble."

Sonora choked on a squeak and fell backwards. For a second, the sun was in her eyes, and then a tall shadow fell across her face and she could see.

It was Adam.

"Darn you," she muttered, as she sat up, then yanked the pole from the water and flung it on the ground. "You scared me."

"Sorry," he said, but he was smiling as he sat down beside her.

"No you're not," she said, and then pointed a finger in his face. "I didn't even hear you coming. How did you do that?"

"I'm Indian."

She rolled her eyes and then punched him lightly on the arm.

"You're full of it, that's what you are."

His smile widened. "Well, there is that, too."

She wanted to stay indignant, but it didn't work.

Adam brushed his hand against the curve of her cheek. "Forgive me?"

His dark eyes were glittering with laughter and his mouth was curved up in a smile. There was a small bead of sweat at the edge of his hairline as well as a sheen from the heat on his face. He smelled good—like the outdoors with a hint of musk, and the look in his eyes was on the broad side of dangerous.

At that moment, Sonora knew if she let it happen, they would be lovers. Part of her wanted to know him in that way. He was kind and generous. She could only imagine what kind of a lover he would be. But she had to remember there was danger in giving too much of herself away, and danger to whomever she let get too close. Buddy's death was evidence of that.

Adam watched the playfulness come and go on her face and wondered what she was thinking, although he doubted she was the kind of woman who gave away her secrets.

"Hey," he said, and playfully bumped his shoulder against hers.

She managed a half-hearted smile and then looked away.

"You're forgiven," she said.

She was slipping away from him and he couldn't let that happen.

"Hey," he said again, and cupped her face with the palm

of his hand, pulling gently until she was looking at him. "What just happened here?"

Sonora met his gaze straight on. "I'm not who you need to be hanging out with."

He inhaled sharply. She was thinking of Buddy Allen.

"I don't run from anything," he said. "Not even you."

Sonora frowned. "I don't know what you think you want, but I'm not it."

"I don't think. I know what I want," Adam said. "I'm just not sure you're ready to hear it."

Sonora's heart skipped a beat.

"I don't run from anything…or anyone…either," she said. "I left Phoenix only because I was ordered to do so."

Adam turned until he was facing her. His legs were crossed, his gaze steady upon her face.

"I know," he said gently. "You are fierce and you are strong. You wouldn't be your father's daughter if you were not. But it's not your job to protect me or Franklin. We've faced our own troubles and dealt with them just fine."

"You've never had troubles like the kind Miguel Garcia can bring."

Adam shook his head, then ran the tip of his finger down her nose, tapping the end like punctuating a sentence.

"Again you forget I was an Army Ranger. I've been in the middle of things the American public never knew happened. I am not afraid of a drug dealer, and you should trust me when I tell you this."

He was no longer smiling, and the tone of his voice was as dark as his eyes. Sonora took a deep breath and then nodded.

"Okay."

Adam hated the expression in her eyes. It was a combi-

nation of distrust and fear. When he reached for her, she
looked away.

"Don't do that," Adam said.

There was a frown on her forehead as she cast a sideways glance.

"I don't know what you are talking about." she asked.

"Are you afraid of what you're feeling?"

Her nostrils flared as she raised her chin. "I still don't
know what you're talking about."

It was a defensive motion Adam knew only too well. He
shook his head, leaned forward, slid a hand behind her neck
and pulled her into a kiss.

She sighed, then she moaned. She'd known this man
would be different. This man could hurt her in a way like no
other. She knew it and still clung to the urgency in his kiss.

Adam had no sense of self. He'd lost it the moment he'd
covered her mouth with his. He'd known it would be like
this. She was sweet as wild honey, but the kiss was no
longer enough. He rose up on his knees without breaking
their kiss, then pulled her up to meet him. Now they were
body to body, clinging to each other in quiet desperation.

The kiss lengthened—deepened.

Sonora lost focus when he took down her hair and ran
his fingers through the length. She swayed weakly, then
grabbed his shoulders to steady herself, but it was too little, too late.

Adam took her in his arms and laid her down, cradling
the back of her head with his hand as he leaned over her,
and as he did, saw a moment of panic on her face. Regret-
fully, he leaned down and rubbed his cheek against her
face. Her skin was warm against his lips, and he could feel
the rocket of her pulse against his fingers.

"I will never hurt you," he whispered.

A tear rolled out of Sonora's eye.

"You will break my heart."

The poignancy in her words was a red light to what had been about to happen. Adam didn't know what to say to make her believe it wasn't true. But he couldn't—wouldn't—make love to her without her complete faith and trust.

"Never," he said softly, then wrapped his arms around her and rolled them both until she was the one on top. They lay without moving or talking while the passion cooled.

Sonora didn't know what to think. She'd thought they were going to make love and she'd wanted it. God knows how bad she'd wanted it. She still ached for the weight of him—for that promise in his eyes of things to come. And she still couldn't believe what she'd said—that he would break her heart. It was as good as admitting that she already cared for him, which seemed ridiculous. They'd spent less than twenty-four hours together, but she felt as if she'd known him forever. He was a healer. Maybe he was a wizard as well.

"Adam?"

He shifted to allow the weight of her head against his shoulder.

"Hmm?"

"Did you really make magic to get me here?"

He sighed. How did you explain the Indian way to someone who had not been raised in the culture.

"It's not magic…exactly."

"Did you put a spell on me, too?"

He grinned. "Honey, I didn't even know you were you until I saw you at the gas station with the fire of a setting sun behind your back. How could I put a spell on someone I'd never met?"

"I don't know…maybe the same way you sent for me. What did you call those…those…?"

"The Old Ones?"

"Yes, the Old Ones."

"Do you believe in them?" he asked.

Sonora rose up on her elbows to look down at his face.

"I don't know what to believe, but I'm here, and that in itself is a miracle. So if I accept your truth of how I got here, then it's not reaching much further to assume you've put a spell on me." She looked embarrassed, but she kept talking, intent on making her point. "It's the only explanation for this…this…thing that's between us."

Adam's eyes narrowed. "It's called sexual attraction."

Her eyes widened. She almost smiled.

"Is that what you call it?"

"Well, woman…it's what we Indians call it. Is there another name for hot and heavy in the white man's world?"

She grinned, then lightly punched his shoulder. "You're teasing me."

He grinned back. "Not about the sex part."

"Okay, so there's something between us."

He arched an eyebrow and rocked his pelvis against her belly. "Yeah, but don't worry. Eventually, it will go away."

This time she laughed out loud then rolled off him and grabbed her fishing pole. "Shut up, Two Eagles. I have fish to catch."

"Can I watch?"

She eyed him cautiously. "Are you capable of keeping your hands to yourself?"

"Oh, yes," he said, and then proceeded to kiss her one more time.

"Hey," Sonora said. "I thought you said—"

"You asked me if I was capable of keeping my hands to

myself. I told you the truth. I am capable. But I didn't promise I would."

Sonora cast the line in the water, then propped the pole against a rock. Without saying a word, she turned around, grabbed Adam by the collar with both hands and yanked him forward.

They'd kissed before, but never like this. Sonora set him on fire. He'd thought about dying plenty of times, but never thought it would be like this.

"Sonora…God…let me—"

She turned him loose as fast as she grabbed him.

"I've got a bite," she said calmly, bent down and picked up her fishing pole and landed a fish.

Adam was still shaking when she took it off the hook and put it on the stringer.

"You'll stay for lunch, won't you?"

Adam took a deep breath and jammed his hands through his hair, but wouldn't answer.

That didn't stop the conversation.

"Good," Sonora said. "How hungry are you…one fish or two?"

"Starving," he muttered, and pulled his T-shirt over his head.

When he sat down and pulled off his boots, then got up and started unbuckling his belt, Sonora's lips went slack.

"Um…uh…"

He glared. "What? Don't tell me you've never seen a naked man before?"

Sonora's mouth went dry. She'd seen naked men before, but never one so remarkably built or so remarkably aroused.

She glared back. "I've seen plenty," she snapped.

"So what's your problem then?" he asked.

She kept trying to look at his face, or at the trees under which they were standing—at anything and everything but the obvious.

"Uh…you're…you're…"

"I'm what?" he said, and then turned his back on her and dived into the water.

She watched the perfect dive with undue appreciation, both for his form and his perfect backside.

He came up with a whoosh, sending a shower of water into the air. The frustration and anger were gone from his face. To add insult to injury, he was treading water and grinning.

Sonora wanted to scream.

"I'm sorry," he said. "I think I was in the water when you answered. You were saying I was…?"

Sonora hadn't grown up alone and tough for nothing.

"I was about to say…you're scaring the fish."

Chapter 9

Sonora made Adam clean the fish. He considered it only fair since he'd come to the meal uninvited. Franklin woke up just as Sonora was taking the last fish from the skillet and followed the scent of his favorite food into the kitchen.

His delight in knowing there was fish for lunch doubled when he realized they would be having company.

"Adam! It's good to see you. I was beginning to think you'd found something better to do than visit a sick old man."

"You're not old," Adam said.

"Maybe not, but today I am not so sick that I can't eat some of this wonderful fish. Daughter! It seems you have been busy while I was sleeping."

"You have no idea," Sonora muttered, then made herself smile.

She was still shocked at herself for letting Adam push all her buttons. Her lack of self-control was so out of character she felt off-center with the world.

Franklin paused. There was something different in her tone of voice, and now that he was looking, there was something different about her appearance as well. This morning her hair had been up. Now it was down, and her face was flushed. The flush on her cheeks could have been from the heat of the kitchen, but the fact that she was studiously avoiding looking at Adam seemed more likely. And, there was no explanation forthcoming as to why Adam's hair was damp.

"Has something been going on in my house that I should know about?" he asked.

Sonora looked guilty.

Adam looked up. "Of course not, Franklin. I would never disrespect you or your home in that manner. The pond, however, is neutral territory, right?"

Sonora gasped, and then glared at Adam all over again.

Adam's eyes were twinkling, but his expression was completely calm as he awaited Franklin's answer.

Franklin grinned. "Yes. You are right. The pond is neutral territory."

"Oh…I'm so laughing my head off," Sonora muttered, then pointed at Adam. "You. Put some ice in the glasses, please."

Adam knew better than to say anything else. He was still reeling from the kiss she'd laid on him down at the pond.

"Hey, Franklin…I was looking at that new piece you're working on. It's really something. What kind of bird is that…a wren?"

"Yes. I thought it was going to be a barn swallow, but when I began carving, the wren is what began to emerge."

Sonora was listening to their conversation with interest as she put a small bowl of quartered lemons on the table, along with a bottle of tartar sauce.

"You mean, you don't know what the sculpture is going to be before you begin?" Sonora asked.

Franklin smiled. It was something people often asked him once they found out his process.

"How can I know until I remove the excess wood?"

Sonora's eyes widened with amazement. "The excess?"

"Yes, you know—the part that doesn't belong."

"That's just amazing," she said.

Franklin shrugged. "It's not so much. It's just the way it works."

A timer went off.

"I'll get it," Adam said.

"It's the cornbread," Sonora said, and pointed to a platter on the counter. "After you cut it, would you put it on that plate?"

Already absorbed in his task, he nodded absently.

Sonora caught herself staring, and when she finally came to herself and turned around, her father was grinning at her.

"Don't say a word," she warned him.

Franklin could tell she was interested in Adam. He just didn't know how much.

It was all Sonora could do to sit down at the table with Adam and get past the memory of his naked body enough to pass him the fried potatoes.

Adam knew she was bothered. It served her right. Yes, he'd kissed her first, but it hadn't been the toe curling, mind-blowing lip lock that she'd laid on him. She was dangerous to mess around with.

Still, he couldn't keep his eyes off of her. There was tension in her shoulders and her back was too straight. She was bothered all right. He smiled as he passed her the bowl of potatoes.

"Want some?" he asked.

Her eyes narrowed. He wasn't asking about potatoes and they both knew it. She snatched the bowl from him and spooned a large helping onto her plate, then passed it to her father.

Adam managed to pretend disinterest as the meal progressed, but the truth was, he could have used another cold dip in the pond.

It wasn't until they were doing the dishes that Franklin decided to stir the pot simmering between his daughter and friend.

"Hey, Adam, isn't there a pow-wow coming up in a couple of weeks at the camp grounds?"

Adam was drying the last plate and answered before he thought. "Yes."

"You gonna go?" Franklin asked.

"What's a pow-wow?" Sonora asked.

"Kind of like a family reunion. There will be food and both men and women's dancing."

Sonora frowned. "What do you mean…men and women's. Don't they dance together?"

"No."

"Isn't that sort of anti-social?"

"Not when you see it," Franklin said.

"Then show me," she said.

Franklin sighed. "I'm sorry, Sonora. I would like to, but I'm afraid I will have to wait and see how I feel when the time comes."

"I could take her," Adam said.

Franklin pretended to think about it, when in fact, it was his plan all along.

"Yes, that might be best," he said. "If I feel well, I can come with you, but if I don't, then you two can go on alone. Would you like to do that, daughter?"

Sonora wanted to know this side of her heritage, but she wasn't sure she'd learn a damn thing with Adam Two Eagles except how much restraint she had left. Still, she wasn't about to let either one of them know how much she wanted to be with Adam.

"Sure. Why not?" she said, then added, "But I hope you can come, too."

"As do I," Franklin said. "It would give me great pleasure to introduce you to some of our clan."

"Clan? You mean the Kiowa?"

"The People are Kiowa, but we are of different clans. We belong to the Snake Clan, as does Adam and his family."

Sonora felt the blood draining from her face and thought she would pass out. There was a roaring in her ears and her legs suddenly went weak.

"Oh, God…oh God," she whispered, and staggered backward. Adam caught her, steadying her until she could sit down in a chair.

"Sonora? What's wrong? Are you ill?" Franklin asked.

Adam knelt down in front of her, then looked up into her face. "Sonora? Sonora?"

She saw Adam's lips moving, but she couldn't hear anything but the thunder of her own heartbeat.

Franklin pulled up a chair and sat down beside her as Adam bolted from the room.

"Daughter…what did I say? If I offended you, it was unintentional."

Adam came back with a wet washcloth and pressed it to Sonora's forehead.

"Here, honey, see if this helps," he said.

She grabbed it with both hands, and then swiped it across her face.

"This just keeps getting crazier and crazier," she muttered. "Half the time I feel like the luckiest woman in the world, and the other half of the time, like I've fallen into the Twilight Zone."

She handed the washcloth to Adam, and then stood abruptly.

"You said you belong to the Snake clan?"

Both men nodded.

"What does that mean?"

Franklin frowned, then looked to Adam for support.

"Think of it like this," Adam said. "You are an American, from the state of Arizona, right?"

"Right."

"So, then transpose that same identification process to your ethnicity. You are Kiowa, from the Snake Clan."

"So, what does the snake mean to people from the same clan?"

"It's like our totem…what the white man might consider a mascot. But we believe it is like a conduit between us and the spirit world. That's a little simplistic, and it means much more, but it's the best way that I can describe it."

"I see," she said, and began rubbing her hands together nervously. "This is so weird," she kept saying.

"What is it that is weird to you?" Franklin asked.

She shrugged and tried to laugh, but it sounded more like a sob.

"Wait until you see this," she said, and stood up, then turned her back on the men.

Before they knew what was happening, she'd pulled her T-shirt over her head, revealing the tattoo of an elongated snake that traced the length of her spine. The snake's tail was somewhere below the waistband of her jeans, while the head marked the bottom of her shoulder blades and was twisted toward the viewer with fangs showing and the forked tongue extended. It was so perfectly depicted that neither man would have been surprised if it had suddenly hissed and struck.

Franklin's eyes widened in disbelief.

Adam inhaled sharply.

"This is strong medicine," he said softly.

"Daughter, how long has this been on your body?"

"Since I was sixteen," she said.

"Your parents let you do this?" Adam asked.

"I didn't have parents, remember. At sixteen, I'd just run away from my third foster home in the same year. I think I was on the streets in San Francisco when I had it done," she said, and pulled her shirt back down before she turned around. "Cost me a whole week's worth of tips, too."

Franklin stifled a moan. There were times when the plight of her childhood took his breath away.

"I'm so sorry," he said softly.

She frowned. "About the tattoo?"

"No, no, that's not what I meant," Franklin said. "When I hear you speaking of your growing up years, it always saddens me. You should have been with family, learning the ways of The People and growing up knowing you were always safe and always loved."

Adam was momentarily stunned to silence. That this woman, who knew nothing of her heritage, should choose such a mark for her body made her powerful. He suspected the Old Ones had always known where she was and were just waiting for the right time to show her the way home.

"Sonora."

She hesitated, then shifted her gaze from her father to Adam. "What?"

"Why the snake?"

"You mean, as opposed to any other tattoo I might have chosen?"

He nodded.

"The reason just sounds silly," she said.

"Try me," he asked.

"Have you ever been in a tattoo parlor?"

He nodded.

"So…you know how they have all these photos and drawings of different tattoos? Well, I was with a couple of friends. We'd been in there for a good hour, looking at photos and daring each other to go first, but no one could decide on what they wanted. I was flipping through this book of drawings and when I got to the page that had this snake on it, I felt like I was going to pass out. The room started spinning around me and I began hearing a rattle in my head…like the kind a rattlesnake makes."

The skin crawled on the back of Adam's neck. The Old Ones had been with her all along and she'd never recognized the signs.

"The tattoo on your back…it's a rattlesnake?" Adam asked.

"Yes. You can't see the rattles unless I'm—"

"Naked," he said, and felt like he'd been punched in the gut.

She nodded, then glanced at her father.

His face was expressionless. She didn't know what he was thinking, but it surely had nothing to do with the tattoo. She'd had the tattoo for so long that she often forgot it was there. Slightly embarrassed, she pulled her shirt back over her head moments before Franklin laid his hand on the top of her head.

"You are blessed among women," he said softly.

She was uncomfortable with what she considered Indian voodoo and tried to make light of it.

"Couldn't prove it by me," she said. "My life has been anything but blessed and pure."

"Not in that way," Adam said. "The snake has power not often given to a woman."

"I don't get it," she said. "I wasn't born with this. It's not a birthmark. It's a tattoo I picked out of a book, compliments of a man named Stumpy."

"You didn't pick it. It chose you," Adam said.

"I don't—"

"You said you heard it rattle?"

"Yes, but Stumpy was smoking weed. We were all probably suffering the effects of his secondhand smoke."

Adam stifled a frown. "Believe what you must."

"Yeah, okay…whatever," she said, a little embarrassed by the seriousness of the conversation.

Franklin kissed the side of her cheek and gave her a quick hug.

"If you don't mind being left on your own again, I think I will go work on my little bird for a while. He's anxious to be free."

"And I need to go check on Linda Billy's little girl," Adam said.

"I hope she hasn't been ill. She's a sweet child," Franklin said.

"Not exactly ill," Adam said. "She overheard her grandmothers talking about someone dying in their sleep. By the time Johnny called me, she'd been awake almost three days."

"Poor baby," Sonora said.

Adam eyed her curiously. "So, Sonora, what are you going to do this afternoon?"

"It's too hot to be outside," Sonora said. "I'm thinking about a nap under the air conditioner in my room."

"Come with me," he said.

"Uh…"

"It's not far. I'll have you back in a couple of hours."

Sonora glanced at her father. "Dad?"

He smiled. "You'll like them."

She still wasn't convinced. "So…what are you going to do there?" she asked.

Adam grinned. "Well, I won't be killing any chickens and slinging the blood about the house or praying to the sun gods today, if that's what you're worried about."

Franklin snorted softly, then grinned.

She glared. "You're making fun of me."

Adam jammed his hands in his pockets and grinned. Payback was fine. "Yeah, I am," he drawled.

"Fine! Laugh your head off while I go change my clothes. I smell like fish."

"Okay, but don't dress up," Adam warned. "The Billy family is a fine family, but somewhat distressed when it comes to money."

"Well, damn, and I had my heart set on wearing the Versace," she snapped, as she strode out of the room.

Adam figured he'd aggravated the situation even more by telling her what to do. The last thing he heard her say was something about "….making me nuts."

He frowned, then let go of regret. He had all afternoon to get her in a good mood.

"I'm going to the studio while I have the energy to work," Franklin said. "It was good to see you. Come back soon."

Adam grinned. "You know I will."

Franklin turned to leave, then paused. "I wish you well," he said softly.

Adam stilled. "Thank you. You honor me with your trust."

Franklin nodded.

"She doesn't need my permission to do anything, but I ask only that you don't hurt her. She's been hurt far too many times already."

"I would sooner hurt myself," Adam promised.

"Then it is done," Franklin said, and walked away, leaving Adam on his own.

He didn't quite know how he felt, but he knew he was more than attracted to Sonora. She did things to him—made him feel things that he'd never felt for another woman.

And there was that tattoo. It had to be more than coincidence that a lost child of the Kiowa would choose the sign of her clan purely by accident. Adam was certain that there was more at work here than either he or Franklin first believed, and he didn't know where he fit in it all. What he did know was that he didn't want to lose the tenuous connection that they had.

"Is this all right?" Sonora said.

Adam turned around, surprised that she had changed clothes so quickly. She was wearing a pair of clean, but well-worn jeans with a denim shirt hanging loose against her hips. It was sleeveless and nearly white from countless washings, but both the jeans and the shirt were clean and crisp. She'd brushed the tangles out of her hair and left it hanging. It swung against her neck as she walked, teasing Adam with its silky sheen.

"Where's Dad?" she asked.

"In the studio."

"Wait. I need to talk to him." She dashed from the room before Adam could answer.

Franklin was already bent over the work table when Sonora hurried inside.

"Dad...I need a favor."

He smiled as he looked up. "After that fine fish dinner...you have but to ask."

"This little girl that we're going to see. How old is she?"

"Not sure...four or five...maybe six. Why?"

"I would like to take her a gift, but I don't have anything. What would you suggest?"

He looked up, quickly scanning the pieces of the shelves of his studio as he moved toward them.

"How about this?" he asked, and lifted a small carving from the end of a shelf, then put it in the palm of her hand.

"Oh, Dad...it's perfect. Do you mind?"

He shook his head as he smiled. "Mind? It is my joy to be able to share my work with you."

She threw her arms around his neck and gave him a quick kiss on the cheek.

"Thank you again," she said, then added, "Don't work too long."

"I'm fine," he said. "I've been taking care of myself for years. I can do it for a while longer, I think."

Sonora frowned as she watched him return to his work table. What he'd said was an unwanted reminder of the limits with which he was living.

"We'll be back soon," she said.

"Take your time," he said, already immersed in his work.

Sonora dropped the carving into her shirt pocket and then ran back into the living room.

"Okay, I'm back," she said. "Are you ready?"

"Oh yeah. I stay ready," Adam answered.

Words stuck in the back of her throat as her mind went right to the memory of him brown and bare as the day he was born. Despite the knot in her belly, she straightened her shoulders and tossed her hair.

"Shut up, Two Eagles, and just so you know...I'm a black belt in Karate."

"Well now...isn't that interesting? I had no idea that we have so much in common."

"What are you talking about?" she asked.

"I'm a black belt, too."

She rolled her eyes.

"Weren't we going somewhere?"

He opened the door and then stepped aside.

"After you, Ms. Jordan."

The ride to the Billy home started out awkwardly, but it wasn't long before Adam had Sonora laughing about an incident from his childhood.

"I can't believe you and your cousin thought up such an intricate revenge."

He laughed as they sped down the road, leaving a cloud of dust behind them to settle on the trees and bushes along the way.

"We were ten. What can I say? Kenny was like a brother to me, and Douglas Winston told all the kids at school that Kenny still wet the bed. We just figured to give him a dose of his own medicine."

"Yes, but how did you get the plastic tube under him while he was sitting at the desk?"

"Douglas had a habit of breaking the lead in his pencils, so he was always having to get up to sharpen it. Kenny sat right behind him and I was on Kenny's right with the aisle between us. We waited until Douglas got up to sharpen his pencil. When he was on the way back, we pretended to be working, and as soon as he turned around and began sitting down, Kenny slipped the tube directly under him. It was so small and pliable that he never felt it. As soon as he began writing again, I handed Kenny the water bottle. He poked the tube in the place where the straw would go, then squeezed. Water went up and through that tube as slick as butter."

"Didn't the other kids see you?"

"Yeah, but Douglas was something of a bully, so they figured he had it coming."

"Then what happened?"

"The bell rang. Kenny yanked the tube out from under him as he leaned over to get his backpack out from under the seat. I stuffed the water bottle in my backpack while Kenny stuffed the tubing in his, and we ran like hell out of the classroom."

"What about Douglas?"

"Well, it looked like he'd peed his pants and then sat in it. We were halfway up the hall when we heard him squall. He bellowed and bawled and then refused to come out of the room. The principal had to call his Mama, who had to take off work to bring him some dry underwear and pants. She was so mad. He begged to go home, but she made him change his clothes and stay."

"Did he ever know it was you and Kenny?"

"Probably, but he didn't have the guts to confront us and everyone was so busy teasing him that they forgot all about Kenny. It was fifth grade justice at its best."

"Remind me never to get on the wrong side of you," Sonora said.

Adam tapped the brakes as he took a sharp turn, then glanced sideways.

"I'll never be your enemy, Sonora. Trust that. Remember that."

Sonora felt branded by the glitter in his eyes, but it was the promise of his words that soothed the fire. Even after he turned his attention back to the road, she kept watching him time and time again. She knew he was right. They'd never be enemies, but they would be lovers. Of that she was certain.

Chapter 10

Clouds were beginning to gather as Adam pulled up in front of Johnny Billy's home. He eyed the sky, remembering that there were thunderstorms predicted for this part of the state later today. From the way they were building, it appeared that they would be here sooner. Still, he believed they had time for him to check on Patricia.

"Do they know you're coming?" Sonora asked.

He nodded.

"Are you sure it's okay that I'm with you?" she added.

He took her by the hand and gave it a tug.

"Yes, I'm sure, and don't try to make me think you're scared of an ordinary family and one little girl...not after I know what you do for a living."

"There's scared and there's scared," she said. "It's far more scary to face rejection than it is to face danger or pain."

Adam was silenced by the simplicity of her words, and

NO POSTAGE
NECESSARY
IF MAILED
IN THE
UNITED STATES

BUSINESS REPLY MAIL

FIRST-CLASS MAIL   PERMIT NO. 717-003   BUFFALO, NY

POSTAGE WILL BE PAID BY ADDRESSEE

SILHOUETTE READER SERVICE
3010 WALDEN AVE
PO BOX 1867
BUFFALO NY 14240-9952

If offer card is missing write to: Silhouette Reader Service, 3010 Walden Ave., P.O. Box 1867, Buffalo NY 14240-1867

Get FREE BOOKS and a FREE GIFT when you play the...

LAS VEGAS

GAME

Just scratch off the gold box with a coin. Then check below to see the gifts you get!

YES! I have scratched off the gold box. Please send me my **2 FREE BOOKS** and **gift for which I qualify.** I understand that I am under no obligation to purchase any books as explained on the back of this card.

▲ DETACH AND MAIL CARD TODAY! ▲

340 SDL D7XX   240 SDL D7YY

FIRST NAME   LAST NAME

ADDRESS

APT.#   CITY

STATE/PROV.   ZIP/POSTAL CODE   (S-IM-10/05)

| 7 | 7 | 7 | Worth TWO FREE BOOKS plus a BONUS Mystery Gift! |

www.eHarlequin.com

| 🍒 | 🍒 | 🍒 | Worth TWO FREE BOOKS! |

| 🔔 | 🔔 | ♣ | TRY AGAIN! |

at the same time, shamed. He'd grown up so confident of his sense of worth. He couldn't imagine what it had taken for Sonora to become the self-possessed woman she was today.

She was a true beauty. Her hair was thick and dark. He liked it when she chose to wear it down as she was today. Her eyes were brown, just like Franklin's, and she had a jut to her chin, just like Franklin, when she was about to defy propriety. Still, he knew that the jut to her chin was also part of the armor she wore to protect her heart. He didn't know what it was going to take to make her trust him, but he was willing to wait.

"So, let's get this show on the road," he said. "The weather doesn't look as promising as it did when we left. We probably won't stay very long."

"I'm lost when it comes to Oklahoma weather, so I bow to your greater understanding," she said.

Adam smiled as he opened the door and got out. Sonora slid out behind him, then followed him to the house. Just as they were walking up the steps, the front door opened. It was Linda Billy.

Adam smiled easily as he gave Sonora's hand a comforting squeeze.

"Hello, Linda."

"Hey, Adam." She glanced shyly at Sonora. "Welcome. Come in, please. It's so hot this afternoon."

Adam put a hand at the small of Sonora's back, and as he did, remembered the snake tattoo. The urge to jerk his hand back was instinctive, even thought it was just a picture on her skin and not the real thing, the power of its presence was not lost on him.

"Johnny still at work?" Adam asked, as they followed Linda into the living room and sat down.

"Yes. He took Eldon Farmer's route for him this morning. Eldon broke his arm last night feeding cows, which means Johnny won't be home until after midnight." Then she gestured toward the sofa. "Please, sit down."

Adam cupped Sonora's elbow. "Thanks, but there's someone I want you to meet first. Linda, this is Franklin Blue Cat's daughter, Sonora Jordan. She's visiting him for a while."

Linda's mouth dropped open. "Uh…I didn't know…I mean…it's very nice to meet you."

"It's nice to meet you, too," Sonora said.

Before Linda had time to say anything about Franklin's bachelor status that might be embarrassing to Sonora, Adam changed the subject.

"How has Patricia been since I made medicine?"

"Good," Linda said.

"Any residual problems with her sleep pattern?" he asked.

"No, and we buried the little pot the next morning as you suggested." The somberness of her expression changed with a soft, easy smile. "She visits the 'grave' every day with fresh flowers, and was so taken with the burial process that she's since buried a dead beetle, a couple of grasshoppers, one of which was unfortunately, still kicking, and a mole that the dogs dug up and killed. I'll be glad when this fixation with death passes."

She looked at Sonora.

"Do you have children?"

"No," Sonora said. "I've never been married."

Linda giggled. "These days that doesn't mean a thing."

Sonora laughed. She liked the young woman with the round face and happy eyes.

"You're right," Sonora said. "Maybe my answer should have been…no, I've never had the urge. However, my dad and Adam are so taken with your daughter, I can't wait to meet her." She touched her pocket, making sure that the piece Franklin had given her was still there. "I brought her a little gift. I hope you don't mind."

Linda's eyes widened with delight. "Of course not, although I warn you, she might be a little shy at first."

"That's okay," Sonora said. "I know how that feels."

There was the sound of running footsteps on the porch, then a squeak as the screen door opened, then banged shut.

"Mama, Mama, is the magic man here?"

Adam grinned.

Linda rolled her eyes in silent apology as her little girl came running into the room.

In one quick scan, Patricia Billy saw Adam, then the stranger, and came to an abrupt stop. The smile disappeared from her face as she ducked her head and scooted to her mother's side.

Adam held out a hand. "Come talk to me a minute," he asked.

The little girl hesitated, but only a moment. She was too curious to stay still. Timidly, she moved to Adam, making sure to keep on the far side of the strange woman.

Adam put an arm around her. "Patricia, you remember Franklin Blue Cat, don't you?"

She frowned. "The man who finds animals in the wood?"

Adam smiled. "Yes, the man who finds animals in the wood. This is his daughter. Her name is Sonora." Then he looked at Sonora. "Sonora, this is my friend, Patricia."

Sonora had little experience with children, but she instinctively knew what not to do, which was overwhelm them by being too loud and too friendly.

"Hello, Patricia. I am happy to meet you."

Patricia scooted a little closer to Adam, but managed to smile.

Sonora dug into her pocket, and pulled out her gift. "I asked my father for a gift to bring to you. He gave me this and said you might like it."

"Wow," Adam said, and meant it, because the small, perfect horse Sonora was holding in the palm of her hand was so lifelike, the mane and tail appeared to be in motion.

"Oh, Sonora, that is a gift far too expensive for a little girl to have," Linda protested.

"No gift is too expensive if it's given in love," Sonora said, and then extended her hand.

The horse was as enticing as Franklin had predicted it would be. Patricia made a sudden switch in loyalties as she slid out from under Adam's arm and moved to in front of Sonora.

"He has no name," Sonora said, and set the horse in the little girl's outstretched hand.

Patricia took it, then turned it over and over, studying it until she seemed to come to some kind of conclusion.

"Yes, he does," she said. "He said it was Thunder."

Adam raised an eyebrow, then grinned at the expression on Linda's face.

"Don't panic," he said. "I once knew such things, too."

No sooner had it been said, then a loud rumble of thunder sounded overhead.

"And, it appears as if the horse's namesake has arrived earlier than predicted. If you don't have any further concerns about Little Bit, here, then I think Sonora and I will make a quick exit. Severe thunderstorms were predicted today, and I don't want to be out on the road when they hit."

"I hear you," Linda said. "My uncle Harmon…"

"…liked watermelon, didn't he?"

Adam knew the story about Harmon Marshall dying in

a tornado and figured that was the last thing Patricia needed to hear.

Linda was slower on the uptake. "Yes…I guess, but I was going to—"

"Little ears, remember?" Adam said.

Linda's eyes widened, and then her shoulders slumped. "I'm sorry, Adam. I don't know what I was thinking."

He touched her arm, smiling as they walked out onto the porch. "It will take time to remember that she's grown up enough to hear what's being said, but not old enough to grasp the entire meaning."

"Yes, yes, of course," Linda said, and blushed as she looked at Sonora. "You must think I'm a terrible mother."

"On the contrary," Sonora said. "I can see what an amazing parent you are. Patricia is a very blessed child to have both parents in her life."

"Franklin didn't know about Sonora until only recently," Adam explained.

Linda's sympathy was immediate. Her dark brown eyes mirrored a quick rush of tears. "Your mother never told you?" she asked.

"My mother…" Sonora stopped. Patricia was staring intently at her. She knelt quickly until she was eye to eye with the little girl, then reached out and tickled her tummy. "My mother wasn't as nice or pretty as yours," she said.

Patricia giggled, and then saw the family cat coming out from under a bush beside the porch.

"Two Toes…look! We have a new friend," she cried, and held up the miniature carving as she bounded off the porch.

As soon as she was out of earshot, Linda turned back to Sonora. "I must apologize. I did not mean to cross-examine you."

Sonora shook her head.

"It's all right. There's no way you could have known," Sonora said. "Truth is, I never knew my mother. She left me on the doorstep of an orphanage."

"I'm sorry," Linda Billy said softly. Before anyone knew what she was doing, she put her arms around Sonora and hugged her, just as she would have any child who'd been hurt.

Sonora rarely allowed people into her personal space and was completely unprepared for being hugged. Still, the woman's touch was gentle and the tears in her eyes were genuine.

"Thanks," Sonora said, and realized that she meant it.

Linda stepped back and then folded her arms across her chest, as if embarrassed that she'd done something so impulsive.

"Welcome home," she said softly.

Sonora felt as if she'd been sucker punched. Her belly knotted. Welcome home? No one had ever said that to her before. She bit the inside of her mouth to keep from crying and then blinked rapidly to clear her vision.

"Yes…well…thank you," she said, as another round of thunder, this one even closer, rippled through the clouds.

Adam cupped Sonora's elbow.

"Storm's getting closer. We'd better be going."

"Come back any time," Linda said.

"Thank you," Sonora said, as she followed Adam off the steps.

Patricia came running around the corner of the house.

"Bye," she yelled, waving the horse in the air. "Thunder says goodbye, too."

Adam waved and laughed while Sonora got into the truck. He slid in beside her, then started the engine just as the first drops of rain began to fall. By the time they reached the main road again, it was pouring.

Adam glanced up at the dark, lowering clouds and then handed Sonora his cell phone.

"Call Franklin. Tell him we're going to my place. I'm thinking we'll need to take shelter soon and it's closer."

She made the call. Franklin answered on the second ring.

"Dad, it's me. We're just now leaving the Billy residence and it's raining really hard. Adam said to tell you that we're going to go to his place to take shelter."

Franklin had been worrying about them ever since they'd begun forecasting weather warnings.

"Thank goodness," Franklin said. "Tell Adam that there are tornado warnings out for this entire area."

Sonora looked nervously up at the sky.

"Adam…Dad says there are tornado warnings for this area."

"I'm not surprised," Adam said. "The clouds don't look good."

The wind was growing stronger. Trees were bending to the force of the wind as rain fell harder. Sonora thought of her father, alone and unwell.

"Are you going to be all right?"

Franklin smiled to himself. He couldn't remember when someone had been concerned about his welfare.

"Yes, daughter. I will be fine. The storm cellar is right beneath the house, remember? I don't even have to go outside."

"Yes, yes, I just wasn't thinking," she said.

Franklin heard the uneasiness in her voice. "It's not easy getting used to worrying about someone else, is it?"

Sonora sighed. "No, it's not."

"I'll be fine. Call me after the storm passes so I'll know that you're both all right."

"Okay."

The line went dead in her ear. She disconnected, then laid the phone in the seat between them.

"Is he all right?" Adam asked.

"Yes. He told us to call after the storm passes."

"Definitely," Adam said, and then flinched when a limb broke off a tree and landed in the road just behind the truck bed. "That was close," he said.

Sonora was white-knuckled and trying not to panic. "Are we in danger?" she asked.

"We're almost home. It'll be okay."

Breath caught in the back of her throat as a strong gust of wind caused Adam's truck to lurch. She tightened her hold on the door handle, but didn't say a word.

Adam was tight-lipped and entirely focused on keeping the truck in the road and moving.

Thunder roared and thumped, reverberating inside the truck to the point that Sonora's ears popped. A second later, lightning struck just to their right, shattering a tree. Wood flew through the air like shrapnel.

"Look out!" Sonora screamed, as a large shard of wood came toward the windshield.

Adam swerved. It hit the side of the truck, then ricocheted into the ditch.

"Okay…okay…I'm thinking this can't be good," Sonora mumbled.

"We're almost home," Adam said.

Moments later, he turned right.

Sonora couldn't see a thing but a solid sheet of horizontal rain and had to trust Adam knew what he was doing. Suddenly she saw the outline of a house. When he drove around it then stopped, she guessed he'd been right.

"We're here," he said. "We're right beside the cellar. Get ready to get out on my side."

"I'm scared," she said, and then didn't believe that had come out of her mouth.

"Just trust me," Adam said, and jumped out of the truck.

Sonora didn't have time to do anything but gasp before he grabbed her hand and dragged her across the seat and out into the storm.

She couldn't see, and didn't know where they were going, but she remembered what Adam had said. Trust me. The way she looked at it, she didn't have any choice.

Seconds later, he stopped.

"Hold on to my belt!" Adam yelled.

She grabbed the back of his belt as he reached for the door. The force of the wind nearly knocked her off her feet. If she hadn't been holding on to him, she would have been gone.

"Adam! Hurry!" she screamed.

She felt the muscles in his back tense, then ripple, as he pulled the door open against the wind.

"Down!" he shouted. "Come around to my right and get in. Eight steps down! Hurry!"

The wind had begun to whine. Sonora didn't hesitate. She ducked her head against the downpour and turned Adam's belt loose. Seconds later, she felt the first step beneath her feet and began counting as she moved down.

The rain was turning to hail. It peppered against her head and back as she went deeper and deeper into the hole. She could hear Adam coming down behind her and tried to hurry. Instead, she stumbled on the last two steps and fell belly down on the cellar floor just as the heavy wooden door fell shut with a loud, solid thunk.

The cellar was dry but dark. She couldn't see them, but she knew she'd made her arms bleed. They were stinging and burning as she rolled over on her back then sat up.

Adam had seen her falling, but hadn't been able to catch her.

"Sonora…honey…are you all right?" Adam cried.

"I think so," she said.

It was still hailing, but from where they were now, the sounds were muffled.

"Don't move," he said. "I have a lantern down here. I'll get us some light."

"Good," Sonora said.

"Don't tell me you're afraid of the dark," Adam said.

"Okay."

He chuckled as he felt along the shelves for the lantern he knew to be there. "Does that mean you are?" he asked.

"Somewhat," Sonora muttered. "Haven't you found that lantern yet?"

Adam frowned. Her voice was shaking.

"I'm sorry, honey," he said softly. "I'm hurrying." Just as he said it, he felt the base beneath his hands. "Here it is…just a second and I'll have it—"

Light bloomed in a corner of the cellar. It was small and yellow, but to Sonora, it was as good as the bright light of day.

At the same time she saw it, Adam saw her. Her elbows were scraped and her chin was trembling. He reached for her and pulled her up and into his arms.

For a moment, neither one of them moved or spoke. Finally, it was Adam who pulled back, and only then to check her injuries.

"I am so sorry," he said, as he pulled her sleeves away from the scrapes on her elbows. "I think I have some first aid stuff down here."

Sonora watched silently as he opened a small plastic box and then dug through the contents. Rainwater had plastered his shirt and jeans to his body. All it did was remind her of what he looked like nude, and that was a vision she didn't need. Not when they were alone and, for the time being, trapped by the storm.

Adam found a tube of antibiotic, but when he turned around, the look on her face stilled his intent. Every stitch of clothing she had on was soaked and molded to her body like a second layer of skin. When she lifted her arms above her head, then twisted her hair into a knot to wring out the excess water, he looked away. He didn't want to think of the thrust of her breasts against the fabric or the outline of her nipples showing through the thin, wet shirt. He didn't want her to feel trapped or threatened, but if she knew what he was thinking, she very likely would.

She moved into the circle of light, then pointed at the ointment.

"Did you find something?" she asked.

Adam looked at her, then sighed. He'd found something all right. A woman capable of stealing his heart.

"Yes, some antibiotic ointment. Would you let me put some on your elbows?"

"Sure," she said. "Maybe it will make them quit stinging."

"I'm so sorry you were hurt," he said.

Sonora snorted softly as she folded her arms to allow him better access to the scrapes. "Getting shot hurts. These are nothing."

Adam's fingers stilled. He tried to form the words to what was running through his mind, but they just wouldn't come out. It wasn't until he'd put the ointment back into the first aid box that he got it said.

"You've been shot?" he asked.

She nodded. "Once in the leg, once in the shoulder."

He'd been a soldier. He'd seen men shot. He'd seen men die. But for some reason, the thought of this woman in that kind of danger made him sick.

"Couldn't you have picked a safer job?"

"Of course, I could have. But I didn't. What's your excuse?"

There was a challenge in her voice he hadn't expected.

"You're right. I'm sorry. It's none of my business."

The cellar door rattled on its hinges.

Both of them flinched and then turned.

"It's holding," Adam said.

Sonora moved to the back of the cellar, then stood against the wall.

"What if it doesn't?"

Adam sighed. He needed to keep his hands off of her, but he could hardly deny the fear he heard in her voice. He followed her to the wall, then stopped, giving her time to adjust to the invasion of her space.

"Come here," he said, and opened his arms.

Sonora shivered. She wanted what he offered. But at what price? Still, when she walked into his arms, it felt right.

"At least I'm not going to be getting you wet," she said, as his arms enfolded her.

"You're shivering," Adam said, as he cupped her head with one hand and settled the other on the small of her back.

"So are you," she said, and wrapped her arms around his waist.

"That's not cold. That's a healthy physical reaction to a pretty woman."

She hid a smile. "You must be pretty hard up to be turned on by someone who looks like a wet rat."

"I'm not touching any part of that comment," Adam said.

Sonora shivered. "God…aren't you cold?" she asked.

But Adam didn't answer. He was listening to something else.

"Listen," he said softly.

Sonora tensed. "What? I don't hear anything."

"Exactly," Adam whispered.

"Is it over?" Sonora asked.

"I don't know. Stay here. I'm going to take a look."

Sonora grabbed his arm. "Adam! Wait! What if it's just a lull? You might get hurt!"

He stopped, then cupped her face and kissed her. The combination of wet skin and the hot blood beneath it made Sonora's knees go weak. When he finally pulled away, they were both breathing hard. He ran his thumb along the curve of her bottom lip as his eyes narrowed.

"Be right back," he promised.

Sonora's stomach knotted as he moved up the steps. When he put his shoulder against the heavy wooden door to push it up, she held her breath, watching as his head cleared the opening.

"Adam?"

"It's okay," he said. "The storm has passed."

She turned out the lantern, then followed him up the steps. Tree limbs were scattered all over the yard, but the house was still standing and except for slight hail damage, his truck was all right, too.

Adam helped her out, then lowered the cellar door before moving toward the house.

"Let's go inside. I need to check windows," Adam said.

Sonora followed him into the house, then stopped just inside the door. He turned around.

"I'll get everything wet," she said.

He held out his arms. "And I won't?"

She shrugged.

"Would you check the kitchen and laundry room while I take the back of the house?" Adam asked.

"Sure," she said, and after he aimed her in the right direction, they parted company.

Sonora heard his footsteps as he moved down the hall and into the bedrooms. She took off her shoes and then headed for the kitchen, dripping water from her clothes as she went.

The windows were closed, and none were broken, although the plants in his backyard had sadly been shredded. She walked out the back door and onto the porch for a better view and was met at the steps by a large cat.

Sonora knelt as the cat came up to her and rubbed his head against her outstretched hand.

"Hey kitty, are you all right?"

Sensing a sympathetic hand, Charlie the cat butted his head against her leg.

"Rowr."

Sonora smiled as she reached down and rubbed him, but when her hand came away bloody, she gasped. "Oh no! You're hurt!"

She picked him up and hurried back into the house with him, calling Adam's name as she went.

He came running. "What's wrong?" Then he saw Charlie. "Hey, I see you met Charlie."

"He's hurt," Sonora said, and held out her hand.

Adam saw the blood and frowned. "Hey, old fella…did you get caught in the storm?"

"Rowrp."

"So, let's see what's happened to you," he said, as he took the cat out of Sonora's arms and carried him to a table by a window in the laundry room.

Sonora followed anxiously.

"His name is Charlie?"

"Yeah," Adam said, as he rolled the old cat onto his back. "Here it is," he said, as he quickly spied the cut. "It's not too deep, but it's jagged. Probably got caught trying to get out of the storm."

"Can you fix him?"

"Sure," he said gently, as he rubbed a thumb under the cat's chin, then scratched his head. "We'll get him fixed up. There's a blue box in that cabinet behind you. Hand it to me, will you?"

Sonora found it quickly and laid it on the table beside the cat, then opened the lid.

"Would you hold Charlie for me while I find what I need?"

Sonora looked anxious.

"Will he bite me?"

"I don't know. Let's ask him," Adam said.

Sonora thought Adam was joking until he bent down and stared right into the cat's face.

"Charlie, this is my friend Sonora. She's going to help me make you feel better, so no bites or scratches, okay?"

Sonora started to grin, but when the cat looked up at her, as if assessing her worth, the smile died on her face.

"Rrrrp."

"Okay then," Adam said. "Good boy."

"What?" Sonora asked.

"You're good to go. Oh…you might like to know that he loves to have his head scratched right behind his ears."

"I can't believe this just happened," she muttered, as she laid a hand on the big cat's head, then gently began to stroke.

Adam hid a smile. Poor Sonora. She had much to learn about the Indian way. Then he heard her crooning sweet words to his cat and sighed. First Charlie. Next it would be himself. It was only a matter of time before they both succumbed.

Chapter 11

The storm had passed just before sunset. Darkness came quickly, leaving the debris in the yard to be dealt with tomorrow. Sonora called Franklin to let him know they were okay.

"Dad…it's me."

Franklin's joy bubbled over into a delighted chuckle.

"What's so funny?" Sonora asked.

"I'm not laughing because anything's funny. I just couldn't hide my delight in hearing those words come out of your mouth."

"What words?"

"Those 'Dad, it's me,' words."

She grinned. "Oh. Yes." Her smile faded slightly. "What's really strange for me is that even though it's only been a short time since we found each other, it all seems so natural."

"We share blood, daughter."

Sonora bit the inside of her mouth, struggling with a sudden need to cry. She'd had a lot of moments like this lately, and was still unprepared for the feelings of vulnerability.

"So, did the storm pass you by?" she asked.

"Yes, I'm fine. How about you and Adam? Did his home suffer any damage?"

"Some, but I'm not sure how much. I'll let you ask him," she said, and handed Adam the phone.

Adam had changed out of his wet clothes earlier and had gone to get a towel to dry his hair when Sonora called Franklin. He came back into the kitchen in time to hear her side of the conversation.

"What is it?" he asked, as he took the phone.

"It's Dad, wanting to know how much damage you had."

"Oh. Okay," Adam said, then covered the phone so that Franklin couldn't hear.

"I laid out some dry clothes for you on my bed. They'll be too big, but they will feel better than what you have on. Bring your own stuff back with you when you come and we'll toss them in the dryer, okay?"

She mouthed a thank you as she left the room.

At that point, Adam turned his attention to the phone. "Franklin…are you all right?"

"Yes. No damage here. Just a lot of water in the creek."

"We had a close call here. Part of the barn roof is gone but the house is still intact. Got a call from Mose and Sheila Roundtree. They said the road between their house and mine was blocked and probably wouldn't be open until morning."

Startled by the news that she'd overheard, Sonora paused in the doorway and turned around, watching Adam's face. As best she could tell, there was no deception in his voice, but if what he was saying was true, then the good news was she'd be staying overnight. The bad news was that she was secretly pleased.

"Don't try to take that old back road," Franklin said. "It's most likely under water."

"Yeah, I agree," Adam said. "I was going to suggest Sonora stay here for the night, then when daylight comes, we'll see where we are with the roads."

"Good," Franklin said. "Have a good evening and tell Sonora I said good night and I'll see you both tomorrow."

"All right. Take care," Adam said, then hung up. When he turned around, Sonora was standing in the doorway— still in her wet clothes. "Is there something wrong with the clothes I laid out?"

"I don't know. I haven't seen them yet," she said, then added, "I heard what you told Dad."

"Yes?"

"I didn't know the roads were blocked."

"Neither did I until I called Mose and Sheila to make sure they were okay. Sheila said there were about four big trees in the road that would have to be cut up and moved before we could pass."

"Oh."

"Franklin said to tell you good night and that he'd see us tomorrow," he added.

"So…I'm spending the night."

Adam grinned. Now he understood what was on her mind.

"Yes, but through no fault of mine, so you can get that look off your face."

"What look?" Sonora said.

"The one where you slit my throat as soon as I close my eyes tonight."

Sonora's eyes narrowed as she eyed him up and down. "That's not murder you see on my face…it's lust."

At the same time Adam's grin died, his belly knotted. "Damn, woman."

"What?" Sonora asked.

"You don't mince words, do you?"

Sonora shrugged. "Waste of time."

"Yeah. Right," Adam said, and then glanced at the clock. "Are you hungry?"

Sonora thought about the next few hours and shivered. Eating seemed like a good idea but she wasn't sure that she'd be able to swallow a bite.

"Maybe," she said. "But nothing difficult. Do you have stuff for sandwiches or some cans of soup?"

"I have both."

"You do soup. I'll make sandwiches," she offered.

"When do we get to the lust?" Adam asked.

Sonora laughed out loud.

Adam didn't.

She frowned. "You're not serious."

"Why not? You were," he said.

"But—"

Adam cupped her face with his hands. "Don't go all female on me. You spoke your mind. I love that about you."

Sonora felt the air go out of her lungs. "You love…?"

He sighed. "Ah, for Pete's sake, Sonora. Don't freak. Consider it a poor choice of words."

"What kind of soup do we have?"

"I am so out of my element here," Adam muttered, as he turned around and strode to the pantry. He turned on the light then stepped aside. "Get out of those wet clothes first before you make yourself sick. As for the pantry…feel free to investigate," he said. "I'm going to feed Charlie." Then he took a small can of cat food from a sack beneath the shelves and left her alone in the kitchen.

Sonora stared at the soup cans as if her life depended on it, when in truth, all she could think about was Adam and the inevitability of sex. Still, the only decision she had to make at the moment was choosing what kind of soup they were going to have with their sandwiches.

She started into the pantry, then remembered she'd been going to change, so she hurried out of the room.

A short while later, Adam heard her banging around the pantry and gritted his teeth. He might not survive this woman, but he was falling under her spell. If he didn't survive, it would be one hell of a way to die. Meanwhile, he had a cat to feed.

Earlier, he'd padded a laundry basket with a handful of old towels to make a bed for the injured cat. He knelt down and pulled Charlie's makeshift bed from under a table, then peered over the side.

Charlie was looking up, somewhat the worse for wear.

"Hey, Charlie," Adam said, as he leaned over and rubbed the old cat's head. "Feeling better now, aren't you?"

He could feel the lack of tension in the cat's muscles, which told him that the pain the cat had been in earlier was easing. Obviously, his medicine was working.

"How about some supper, fella?"

"Meowp."

"That's what I thought," Adam said, and emptied the can of cat food onto a paper plate before setting it inside Charlie's temporary bed.

He sat, watching Charlie eat and listening to the sounds of a woman in his kitchen. After a while, he decided he couldn't remember a time when he'd felt this peaceful.

Sonora cut the last sandwich into halves and then laid it on the plate with the others. She hadn't been able to find two cans of the same kind of soup, so she'd made potato soup on her own. It was being kept warm on the back burner while she finished the rest of their meal.

The clothes he'd laid out for her to wear were definitely roomy, but they were warm and dry and she couldn't ask for more. The sweatpants had a drawstring tie to help hold them up and the T-shirt he'd given her was soft from countless washings. He'd left her some socks as well, but she'd chosen to go barefoot instead, and was enjoying the cool surface of the vinyl flooring beneath her feet as she moved about the kitchen.

She knew she'd pushed more of Adam's buttons and wondered what it was about him that made her do that. Normally, she wasn't a confrontational kind of woman, except on the job, but there was something about him that made her nervous.

Maybe after they had sex and got it out of their systems, they wouldn't be so focused on pretending they weren't attracted to each other.

As she finished setting the table, she kept thinking about Miguel Garcia—wondering where the DEA was with regards to his capture and wondering what her life would be like if they never did get him. She didn't know what she thought about spending the rest of her life looking over her shoulder, or fearing what might happen to Franklin or Adam if Garcia knew how much they'd come to mean to her.

She set the last of the cutlery by the bowls and plates then stepped back, eyeing the table to see if there was something she'd missed. Confident that everything was in place, she glanced toward the closed door to the laundry room. Surely Adam was through feeding his cat.

She peered out a window into the darkness, absently hoping she hadn't aggravated him to the point of wishing she wasn't here. Still, he was the one who'd wanted her to go with him, and she wasn't responsible for the weather. The way she looked at it, he was the reason she'd gone, so he didn't have anything to complain about.

Just as she turned back toward the sink, the door to the laundry room opened.

"Something smells good," Adam said.

The fact that he seemed ready to call a truce made her smile.

"It's just potato soup," she said. "I hope you like it."

His eyes widened in delight. "You made soup?"

She nodded.

"From scratch?"

"Yes. You didn't have two cans of soup that were alike so rather than heat up two different kinds, I just—"

Adam hugged her. "After what I've put you through today, you're amazing. I bring you into my house as a guest, not to cook. Still, I confess that I'm looking forward to eating your soup. It's one of my favorites."

Sonora was still smiling when he moved to the kitchen sink to wash his hands. She carried the soup pot to the table and ladled soup into two bowls, then started back to the stove.

"Here, let me," Adam said, and took the pot from her hands and set it on the burner. "Anything else you need?"

Just you. Luckily for Sonora, Adam couldn't read her mind. "No. That's it," she said.

"Then we eat."

Adam seated her, then himself. Once seated, he looked across the table. The feeling of peace that was with him settled firmer. Seeing Sonora at his table seemed so right.

"Ham sandwich?" Sonora asked.

Adam blinked. She was holding the platter.

"Yes, please," he said, and so the meal began.

Sonora was still curious about Adam, and after a few bites of sandwich and part of her soup, she quit eating, put her elbows on the table, and leaned forward.

"Adam?"

He looked up, still chewing. "Hmm?"

"Are your parents still living?"

He nodded as he swallowed quickly. "Yes. They live in Anadarko."

"So, how did you wind up here after you left the army?"

"Oh. This is the family home. I bought it from Mom and Dad after I quit the military. My sister and her family live in Anadarko. Mom and Dad got lonesome for their grandchildren…said they didn't see them enough, and moved. This house had been vacant almost a year when I came back."

"You didn't want to be close to them?" she asked.

He smiled. "It wasn't that. It was just that I knew what I wanted to do and the people who needed me most were here."

Her eyes narrowed as she tried to picture this brownskinned man with a military haircut and a gun in his hand. He seemed more of a pacifist.

"How did you know…I mean…how did you go from the white man's army to the Indian world without complications?"

"I didn't. The complications were there. Sometimes they're still there, especially with the tribe elders. They see me as something of a contradiction. In my heart, I am a healer, but my past is all mixed up with the white man's conflicts and war."

"Does your past trouble you?" she asked.

"No. It's something I did. It made me stronger, I think, but it didn't lessen my abilities as a healer."

Her eyes narrowed slightly. "How did you know?"

"Know what?" Adam asked.

"That you were supposed to be a healer?"

His expression softened and he almost smiled. "How did you come to law enforcement?"

Sonora frowned. "That's not fair. I asked first."

Adam stifled a grin. "That you did." Then he sighed. "I've always known what I was born to do. I just resisted it for a while."

Her eyes widened. "You knew? How did you know?"

"When I was a child, I got blood poisoning in my foot from stepping on a rusty nail. I was sick for a long time. One night, I heard my parents talking with the doctor. He told them that I might die. I remember being scared...afraid to close my eyes for fear I wouldn't wake up. I think that's why I was so sympathetic with the little girl we went to see today. I remembered what it felt like to be afraid to close my eyes."

"So what happened?" Sonora asked.

He smiled. "Eventually, I slept, but when I did, the Old Ones came to me in my sleep and told me that I wouldn't die because when I grew up, I was going to be a healer."

Sonora's lips went slack as a shiver went up her spine. Even as Adam was speaking, her mind took her straight back to her childhood—to the countless nights she'd gone to bed lonely and afraid only to be visited by a repetitive dream that had both confused and comforted. Surely it couldn't be the same.

Adam saw her reaction and frowned. "What?"

Sonora thought of the tattoo on her back and shivered again.

"What did the Old Ones look like?" she asked.

Adam's frown deepened. There was more than curiosity in her questions, and because of that, he described something that, in another set of circumstances, he would never have revealed.

"They are four ancient warriors. One wears a long war bonnet. Another is wrapped in a bear skin and has the mark of a claw on his chest. The third—"

"What are they riding?" she asked.

He frowned. How did she know there were horses?

"They are riding—"

Sonora shuddered, closed her eyes and finished his sentence. "…ghost horses with red eyes and feathers tied in their manes. One has a black handprint on its left hip. Its rider has two white handprints on his face. The last rider is naked with hair so long that it's tangled up in the mane and tail of his horse."

The hair stood on the back of Adam's neck. "How do you know this?"

"I used to dream about them all the time," she whispered, and then covered her face with her hands. "I didn't know who they were."

Adam stared at her, absorbing the shock of what she was saying. From the time he'd learned of the snake tattoo on her back, he'd believed she was special. This only confirmed it for him. He didn't know what it was she'd been singled out to do, but it was obvious that the Old Ones had a hand in it.

He leaned across the table and pulled her hands from her face. "Sonora. Look at me."

She opened her eyes and found herself falling into the bottomless shadows in Adam's eyes. She felt humbled and at the same time, strengthened by his presence.

"Don't be afraid of your blessings," Adam said.

"Is that what they are?"

Adam sighed. "Why is it so hard for you to understand?"

"If I was so damned special, then why was my childhood staged in the pit of hell? If these Indian…ghosts…were watching over me, as you suggest, then why didn't they help me?"

"How do you know they didn't?" Adam asked. "You're alive."

Sonora went still. Suddenly, all the times she'd walked away from danger without a scratch seemed to be more than what she used to call luck. All the times growing up when she could have been hurt—when she might have been arrested or killed now took on a different tone. Her perceptions of her past took a one-eighty turn. Could this be? Had she been looking at a half-empty glass instead of one that was half-full? It was something to consider.

"You're right. I am," she said. "And my soup is getting cold."

Adam didn't push her into any more conversation. It was obvious that, for the moment, more had been said than she could handle.

"That soup is also wonderful," Adam said softly. "My mother always puts grated carrot with the celery and onion, too. She says that, without it, potato soup is too white."

Sonora laughed.

"You should do that more often," Adam said, then downed his last bite of sandwich.

"Do what?" Sonora asked.

"Laugh," Adam said, talking around a mouthful. He got up from the table, refilled his glass with iced tea and then took a big drink. "Want a refill?" he asked, as he pointed at her glass.

"No. I'm good."

He grinned. "You sure are."

She laughed again. "Are you flirting with me?"

"Yes," Adam said, then took another drink.

Sonora swallowed nervously and then began gathering up the dirty dishes and carried them to the sink.

Adam helped her clean up the kitchen, making small talk when the silence in the room grew noticeable. Finally, he pronounced the room clean.

"That's good enough," Adam said, as he took the dish cloth from Sonora's hands and hung it up to dry. "Don't get it too clean or you'll make my efforts at housekeeping look bad."

"But I just—"

"Sonora."

She sighed, then grew quiet before asking, "It's time, isn't it."

Adam slid his hands around her waist, then stopped without pulling her close. "You're calling the shots," he said softly.

She was still thinking about the power he'd given her when the lights flickered then went out.

"Damn," Adam muttered. "I wondered when that would happen."

Sonora clutched his forearms, telling herself it was okay, that there was nothing in the dark that hadn't been there in the light. Still, her heartbeat accelerated and her knees went weak.

"When what would happen?" Sonora asked. "Aren't they coming back on?"

"Not for a while, honey. Maybe not until morning. Storms are always knocking out power around here. A tree probably fell over on a line somewhere. It will take the power crews a while to find it, then fix it."

"Oh Lord," Sonora muttered.

It was then Adam remembered she was afraid of the dark. He pulled her close beneath the shelter of his arm.

"Honey…I'm sorry. You'll be okay, I promise."

An encroaching panic left her breathless. "Do you have a candle or a flashlight? We need to make light. Please, Adam, we need to make light."

He frowned at the fear in her voice and wondered what had happened to her to make her this afraid.

"And we will. Take hold of my hand. There's a flashlight in my bedroom."

She clung to his hand as if it was her lifeline to sanity. Even though she knew it was Adam who was beside her, her mind wouldn't turn loose from the past—to the foster parent who'd locked her in a closet every time her men friends came calling.

Adam was hurrying. He could tell she was bordering on panic, and while he didn't understand what drove it, he understood fear.

"I've got you, honey. Just hang on to me. We're almost there. I've got a great big flashlight in the table by the bed and there are some candles all around the house. We'll light the place up like a church on Christmas, okay?"

"Okay…okay, just like Christmas."

She tried to laugh, but it sounded more like a sob. God, she hated herself for this weakness. All these years and it was the one thing she'd never been able to get over.

"We're in the bedroom now. Here…feel the bedpost. I want you to sit on the bed while I find the flashlight, okay?"

"Yes. I'm sorry that I'm such a nut case," Sonora said as she sat down on the end of the bed, clutching the bedpost for security.

"You're nothing of the kind," Adam said, as he scrambled for the table. Within seconds, his fingers curled around the handle of the battery powered lantern. "Bingo," he said, and flipped on the light.

Once again, Sonora's world centered.

"Thank God," she muttered, then shook the hair back from her face and stood. "What can I help you do?"

Adam was already pulling a smaller flashlight from a dresser drawer. "I'm going to light a few candles so that we can move around as needed. You can either come with me or wait for me to come back. I won't be long."

"I'll wait."

Adam's cursory glance was meant to appear casual, but he was, in fact, assessing her condition. Even in the poor lighting, the pallor in her face was still evident, but he could tell she was breathing easier from the rise and fall of her breasts.

"I'll be right back."

He took the other flashlight and made a run through the house, lighting candles and moving them about so that there was at least one light in every room in the house. He checked on his cat one last time, satisfied that Charlie was comfortable and sleeping, then locked up as he moved back through the house.

When he got back to his bedroom, Sonora was right where he'd left her, clutching the flashlight and staring into the shadows about the room.

He pulled a couple of Yankee candles from a cupboard and lit them, putting one on the dresser and the other in the adjoining bathroom, then sat down on the bed beside her.

"Sonora…honey…"

"What?"

He put his arm around her shoulders. "I want you to do something for me."

She looked up, then into his eyes and wondered when she'd come to trust him. "What is it?" she asked.

He put his hands on either side of her face and held her

until her gaze was locked into his, then he took one of her hands and laid it on his chest. "Do you feel that?" he asked.

"What…your heartbeat?"

"Yes."

"Yes, I feel it."

Then he put his hand behind her head and pulled until the side of her face was against his chest. "Do you hear it?"

Sonora sighed. The rock-steady rhythm of his heart was impossible to miss. "I hear it," she whispered.

"Then remember, because even if you can't see me, you need to know that, even if the batteries go dead and the candles burn out, I'll be your light in the dark. All you have to do is reach out and I'll be there. Can you remember to do that? Can you remember not to be afraid?"

She nodded.

Long silent moments passed. Moments in which they grew easier with each other's presence. Moments in which Sonora's last hesitation for what was about to occur finally died.

She pulled back from Adam's embrace and then stood. As he watched, she stepped back from the bed and then pulled the borrowed T-shirt over her head.

Adam grunted softly, as if he'd been kicked in the gut, but he never moved.

Sonora untied the drawstring on the sweatpants. They slid from her slender hips into a puddle of fabric at her feet, leaving her completely naked.

It was obvious to Adam that she was comfortable with her body, as she should have been. She was all lean muscle with a soft, womanly shape. When she lifted her arms to take down her hair, he stood.

"Wait," he begged. "Let me."

Without thinking, she turned around, giving him easier

access to the ponytail. But it wasn't her hair that caught Adam's eye. It was the snake tattoo that ran the length of her spine.

He knew she was waiting, but he was unable to move. The snake's eyes seemed to be watching him—marking the distance between them.

Without warning, Adam heard a distant rumble and for a moment, thought another round of thunderstorms were coming. When he realized it was drums he was hearing, the room in which they were standing began to fade and another image soon took its place.

They were standing in a desert with nothing in sight but a distant cloud of dust. Sonora seemed to be swaying to a rhythm only she could hear, while the snake on her back came alive. As Adam watched, the snake slithered off her skin and onto the earth. Then it raised its head toward the dust cloud and began to grow tall. It grew in size until it was standing taller than a tree, directly between them and the approaching cloud of dust.

As the snake grew tall, Sonora seemed to waver, then fell. Adam tried to move, but when he looked down, roots were growing out of his feet into the earth, rendering him immobile.

The dust cloud was closer now, and Adam thought he heard screams coming out of the mass. He didn't know what it was in the cloud, but he knew it meant danger to Sonora. Sweat broke out on his skin as he struggled to get free, but the roots had gone too deep.

Just before the cloud enveloped them, he screamed out her name, and as he did, the snake opened its mouth. In the same moment, Sonora rose up from the ground. There was a split second in Adam's mind when Sonora and the snake seemed to be one. The snake—or Sonora—or maybe it was both—inhaled for what seemed like forever, until they had swallowed the dust cloud whole.

When Adam looked again, the roots were gone from his feet and Sonora was lying motionless on the ground. His heart seemed to stop as fear enveloped him. It couldn't be. He couldn't lose her this way. The snake's rattles were loud in his ear as he called out her name.

Sonora turned around.

"Adam?"

Between one heartbeat and the next, the desert disappeared and Adam was back in his bedroom.

He gasped, as if he'd been drowning, and then staggered backward and sat down on a bench without taking his gaze from her face.

Sonora frowned. "Are you all right?" she asked.

For the moment, speech was impossible. He managed a nod.

"Look, if this isn't the right—"

He pulled her to him, and then buried his face against her belly. Even as he was wrapping his arms around her waist, the sound of rattles was fading from his mind.

She was real. Not the vision. Just her. But as he was mapping the contours of her hips with the palms of his hands, he was certain of one thing. Sonora was in danger, and he wasn't going to be able to do a damned thing about it. Only the power within her was going to keep her alive.

Chapter 12

Sonora knew something had happened. She could tell by the look on Adam's face that it had undone him, but she didn't know what or why. So, when he wrapped his arms around her, she took it as the opening she'd been waiting for, combed her fingers through his hair, then arched her back.

"Come to bed with me, Adam. Make the dark in my world go away."

It was exactly what Adam needed to get the picture of her in danger out of his head. With one motion, she was in his arms and then he was carrying her to the bed. He laid her down, then stripped without word or explanation for what he'd seen. She'd asked him to bed and he wasn't about to refuse.

Once his clothes were off, he paused to look at her, naked in his bed and wanting him. It was something out of a dream.

When she reached for him, he reacted instantly by lying down beside her and taking her in his arms.

When she began to run her hands upon his body, he didn't trust his self-control enough to allow her the freedom. Instead, he swung a leg over the lower half of her body, then straddled her, pinning her to the bed.

"Who do you see?" he asked.

His hair had fallen down on either side of his neck, partially hiding his face from view, and even though they'd never been this close or this intimate, it seemed that she'd known him forever.

"I see you," she whispered, and spread her legs.

Adam's pulse shifted into a higher gear. Her invitation was impossible to misunderstand. He slid into the valley between her thighs, rocking against her a couple of times without penetration, testing his own willpower while waiting for a positive invitation.

"Who am I?" he asked.

"The man I want."

She locked her legs around his back, caught him on a downward thrust and pulled him in.

The joining was immediate, and at the same time, Sonora felt a physical shock, as if she'd touched a live electric wire. She shuddered as she closed her eyes, and still she saw Adam's face, silhouetted against a shower of sparks.

"Don't close your eyes."

His demand seemed impossible to heed and yet somehow, Sonora managed to focus. She saw him, and she saw herself. In a way, it seemed as if time stopped and she was outside her own body, watching them make love. They rocked and writhed in perfect unison, while the shadows from the lamplight flickered upon the walls. Soft whispers, coupled with a moan and the occasional sigh played an accompaniment to the dance.

Sonora was caught up in the act of making love in a way

she'd never known before. Her sense of self was gone, leaving her at the mercy of this man and his skill at bringing her to a frenzy.

She wanted—needed—begged.

He heard her—felt her desperation—matched it with need of his own. Being inside her was like being caught in the storm they'd endured earlier. It was happening, and they were in it together, but without any control.

One moment she was caught up in the power between them and the next she was coming apart. The wave of the climax washed through her so hard that she heard herself scream.

The sound ripped through Adam like a bullet through flesh, shattering mind and body alike as he climaxed along with her.

Coming down from the high they'd created left them both exhausted and breathless, but there was a peace inside Adam that he hadn't felt since he'd come home from the army. Whatever there was between him and Sonora, he wasn't willing to lose it. Gently, he wrapped his arms around her and rolled, so that she was now the one on top.

Sonora lay sprawled across his chest, her long legs entwined with his, her fingers tangled in his hair. There were unashamed tears on her cheeks and a flush to her skin. She felt as if she'd been in a flash fire and cleansed by the heat.

All of the ugliness and the loneliness of her past had been reduced to ashes by this man and what they'd done together.

Slowly, she raised up on her elbows and looked down at him, marveling at the gentleness in his eyes and remembering the passion with which they'd made love. Somewhere between the bed and the moment he'd taken her, the act of sex had been replaced by something more. There had been men in her life before Adam, but there would never be another after him. She didn't know what he hoped to gain from being with her, but she knew what she wanted from it.

She wanted him.

Gently, she traced the dark wings of his eyebrows with her fingertips and kissed the shadows his lashes left on his cheeks. She could feel the faint ebb and flow of his breath from his slightly parted lips and shivered, remembering that he'd actually made her scream.

"Adam…"

His nostrils flared.

"Don't say it," he said. "No promises are needed. Not now. Later, when you come to know and accept that you are forever safe with me, there will be promises made. But not now. Just know that you are in my heart and in my blood."

Sonora's lips parted and she started to speak, then stopped. He was right. For now, all they needed to do was savor the magic they made together.

"All right. But…I have one thing to say."

He smiled. "Of course you do. You're a woman aren't you? Women always have to have the last word."

"Then let me have it," she said, and when he grinned, she laid her hand on his chest. "I see you, Adam Two Eagles. Do you see me?"

Adam was shocked by quick tears that blurred his own vision. Showing emotion, let alone feeling it like this, was foreign to him. He groaned beneath his breath as he reached for her.

"See you? Woman…I am numb to everything but your touch. I don't know what's happening between us, but I am forever changed by what we've done."

Sonora raised up and then sat, straddling his thighs. Adam lay silently, watching the play of light and shadows flickering upon her body from the candles.

Slowly, he watched her as she rocked back on her heels and began stroking him, gently at first and then faster and faster until he was rock hard and aching for a release. It was then that she raised up and took him inside her.

Time ceased. Life shrank to a pinpoint of promised ecstasy as she swung her hair away from her face, arched her back, then bore down, racing with Adam to the end of the dance.

Later, when they could move without shaking, Sonora rolled over onto her side. Adam curled up behind her, pulled the covers over them and held her while she slept.

He watched the shadows lengthen throughout the night as the candles finally burned out, and daylight was only a whisper away. He watched her sleeping while morning broke and drowned the darkness in a fine display of pale light. He watched and remembered his vision and knew that there would come a day when she would need him and he would be helpless to come to her aid. It was the worst thing he'd ever faced—worse than anything the army had ever thrown at him—worse than believing his own life might end. He didn't know the face that danger would wear for her, but he knew it was coming.

Miguel Garcia was, as the cowboys used to say, laying low. The men who'd been sent out to search for Sonora Jordan were making progress, but mostly by elimination. He didn't know where Sonora Jordan was, but he knew where she wasn't, and he knew where she'd been.

There had been two separate sightings of women they thought were the female agent, but both had proved to be mistaken identities. He was frustrated at having to hide in a country that was not his own, and absolutely convinced that he'd been betrayed by someone he trusted. There was no other explanation for how the DEA knew what he was driving and how long he'd been in the States. He'd thought about it long and hard and the only name that kept coming to mind was Jorge Diaz. It seemed impossible to believe that the man who'd helped him escape was the same man who'd betrayed him. There was, however, one way to find out and it meant another call to Emilio Rojas.

Rojas was sitting in a lounge chair under a pair of palm trees holding his newest grandson. The day was hot and sunny in Juarez, just the way he liked it. The baby was his twelfth grandchild, but the first one who had been named for him. Family had gathered for a Sunday meal after church and Emilio was counting his blessings as he held the month-old baby boy.

A peacock was perched on a low limb nearby, emitting intermittent squawks of disapproval for the fact that the yard it normally occupied was full of running, squealing children.

Emilio was laughing and urging on the games that the children were playing, when he looked up and saw his oldest daughter, Pia, coming toward him carrying the phone.

"Papa, it is for you," she said, handed him the phone and took the grandchild out of his arms.

With a few quick words, she ushered the children to another part of the yard to give Emilio some privacy to take his call.

Emilio was not all that happy with the interruption, and after he recognized the caller, even more displeased.

"Miguel, why are you calling?" he asked abruptly.

Miguel frowned. "I have another favor to ask of you."

Emilio stifled a curse. He was old. He was tired. He didn't want anything more to do with the drug world, but it was easier said than done.

"And what would that be?" Emilio asked.

"I have reason to believe that Jorge Diaz is the one responsible for betraying me to the authorities."

Emilio sighed. He knew what was coming, even before Miguel got it said.

"So, how do you know this?" he asked.

"Process of elimination," Miguel said.

"And what do you want me to do about it?" Emilio asked.

"I want Diaz confronted and I want the truth. I don't care what has to be done to make him talk, but if I'm right and he does confess. I want him to pay."

A tiny, dark-eyed, dark-haired toddler crawled up in Emilio's lap just as Miguel was still talking. Emilio's expression darkened. How dare that man talk about such things on a Sunday, and when his family was here! It made Emilio feel obscene to have this precious little face looking up at him with love, completely unaware of what was being said in her presence.

"I am too old for such things," Emilio said.

Miguel cursed. "I need this done," he said. "I can't let it become common knowledge that I was betrayed and let it pass. I want justice. I want him dead."

"Papa…Papa…a candy, *por favor?*"

Emilio stared down at his little granddaughter. She wanted a piece of candy and Miguel Garcia wanted him to kill. If he could have put his hands on Garcia, it would be him who'd be dead.

"Una momento, chica," he said gently, then gripped the phone a little tighter. "Miguel! You know this is no longer my life and yet you ask it anyway?"

Miguel could tell his father's old friend was angry, but he didn't much care. He was the one with problems.

"You know what I'm going through," Miguel said. "I need you to do this for me."

"And what if you're wrong? What if Diaz is not your enemy?"

"Then you find out who is and deal with it!" Miguel demanded.

Emilio gritted his teeth. He knew who needed to be dealt with, but even he didn't have the guts to make an enemy of Miguel. It was his private opinion that Miguel's father had catered to his sons to the point of ruination, but since his old friend was dead and Miguel was the last of the seed, he didn't want the bad karma of being the one who ended the lineage.

"I will do what I can," Emilio said, and hung up before Miguel could argue further, then made a call to his eldest son.

"Benecio, I need a favor."

Benecio Rojas smiled to himself. His father always prefaced his calls with those words.

"What can I do for you, Papa?"

"Find Jorge Diaz and confirm that he's the one who betrayed Miguel."

Benecio frowned. "Then what?"

"You know what," Emilio said.

"Papa, why are we involving ourselves with Miguel's business? You know what he's like."

"Yes, I do," Emilio said. "And for that reason alone, I do it. I don't want a member of my family to go missing because I displeased him in some way."

Benecio cursed beneath his breath, but he understood. "I will do it, Papa, but only for you. Not because I care what happens to Miguel Garcia."

"Thank you, my son. Go with God."

"And you, too, Papa."

Emilio heard his son disconnect, then sighed. He looked down into the little girl's smiling face, laid down the phone, picked her up in his arms and then stood.

"Now, *niña,* let's go find that candy, okay?"

It was Monday, which was why Ming, the Chinese manicurist, was massaging Jorge's right hand while the left hand was still soaking. Ming had fastened a hot pink cape around his neck to protect his clothes and rolled his pants up to his knees while his feet were soaking in a foot bath attached to the massage/manicure chair. The chair was a little cheesy, but Jorge secretly loved the fact that he got a quickie back massage without getting naked.

Actually, Jorge got a manicure and pedicure at Ming's shop every Monday and a haircut every other week at her salon next door. His eyes were closed as Ming turned off the foot bath and wrapped his feet in a warm towel. Part of his mind was savoring his time with Ming, while he was giving himself a mental pat on the back for enlarging his territory, and at the same time, getting rid of Miguel.

He heard the little bell jingling over the front door of the shop, but didn't bother to look up. People came and went in here constantly, and besides that, he was operating on the theory that if he didn't see who'd come in, then he wouldn't have to acknowledge them.

There was also a part of him that thought getting manicures was effeminate, so he didn't want to see judgment in their eyes. The only men he knew who did it were wealthy, thus, the reason for his habit. He wanted the world to know how he'd risen in society. Thanks to the nation's desire for drugs, he was, by anyone's measure, an im-

mensely wealthy man. It suited him to flaunt that, but only
to a degree. Too much attention could get a man in his business killed.

However, once Garcia was completely out of the picture, his wealth would most likely triple. It was only a
matter of time before the DEA found Garcia, and when
they did, he would bet his own life that Miguel would die
before being taken alive—which was exactly what he was
hoping for.

"Mr. D…do you want clear polish on your nails?"

"Sure…why not?" he said.

Ming picked up a bottle of clear polish, tapped it a few
times in the palm of her hand, unscrewed the lid and then
sat it down beside her. She picked up a towel then dried
Jorge's hands thoroughly before loading her nail brush
with polish.

Jorge was pleasantly aware of the scent of sandalwood
as Ming bent her head to her task. He was not aware of the
man with the gun until he felt the barrel in his ear.

"Don't move," the man said softly. "I have a question
for you."

Ming started to quietly weep.

To Jorge, it was more frightening than if she'd been
screaming her head off. Even though he was shocked, it
wasn't entirely unexpected. The lifestyle had its draw-
backs and this was one of them. Only this time he was
wearing Ming's hot pink cape. It was perfect protection as
he opened his eyes and slid his hand inside his jacket.

"Who sent you?" Jorge asked.

The man leaned over and whispered a name in Jorge's ear.

Jorge's face paled. He didn't even need to ask—he already knew the answer. Obviously, Miguel Garcia had
figured out who'd betrayed him. Then he reassured him-

self that it didn't matter. He was here. Miguel was stranded in the States with the American Federales on his trail.

"So…when you get to hell, say hello to his brother for me," Jorge said.

The man's eyes widened in sudden understanding as the protruding bulge beneath the cape around Jorge Diaz's neck suddenly bloomed before he could get off a shot.

The bullet caught Emilio Rojas's oldest son right between the eyes. His blood splattered all over the glass partition behind him, as well as on Jorge and Ming.

Customers were screaming and running with hot pink capes flying and stringing wet nail polish as they went. Ming's hands were over her face and she was wailing in Chinese.

Jorge sighed. Damn. He was probably going to have to find another manicurist. Chances were Ming wouldn't let him in the front door after this. Still, there were things to be done. He grabbed Ming by the shoulder and shook her.

"Ming! Stop crying and call the police. Someone just tried to kill us and I saved our lives."

Even in her shock and fear, she got the message. By the time the Mexican police came, she was all about the man coming in threatening to kill everyone in sight and praising Mr. Diaz for saving their lives.

The police weren't stupid. They recognized Emilio Rojas's eldest son lying dead on the floor, and they knew Jorge Diaz's reputation well. But it was to their advantage not to make waves in this case. The way they figured it, the cartel was just taking care of their own business.

However, no one had taken Emilio Rojas's reaction into account. Before the sun set on the day, every member of Jorge Diaz's family was dead, including Diaz, except his mother, Amelia, who now lived in a sanatorium and hadn't known her own name for the past five years.

Retribution had been met for Miguel Garcia, but at a terrible expense to the Rojas family. And, Emilio had vowed to his family and to himself that if Garcia somehow escaped the talons of the American DEA, he would not escape Rojas, himself.

Miguel continued to live low-key in a Tulsa motel, completely unaware of what had happened, or that Rojas had called in the men who'd been helping him. He didn't know it yet, but he was as alone in the world as he'd ever been. It would be the first time in his life that money wouldn't buy him what he wanted.

Dave Wills was eating breakfast in an IHOP restaurant after an all-night stake-out to nab Garcia. Unfortunately, their tip was wonky. A man named Miguel Garcia had recently arrived in Amarillo flashing a big bankroll, but when Garcia finally showed up at his motel, they discovered it was the wrong man.

The DEA agents were decidedly disgusted with the motel owner who'd called in the tip. After further questioning, he finally admitted that all Mexicans looked alike to him.

Dave had resisted the urge to punch the man out and settled for treating himself to a real, sit-down breakfast instead of sausage, egg and biscuits on the go. He was down to his last few bites of blueberry pancakes and last piece of bacon when his cell phone rang.

He glanced at the caller ID and then answered quickly. "Good morning, sir."

Gerald Mynton grunted a response. After the news he'd just received, it was all he could manage.

Dave could tell something was wrong and glanced down

at his plate, guessing his appetite was about to change. "Sir, do we have a problem?"

"You might say that," Mynton said. "I've got a call in to Sonora, but she has yet to return it. I'm not sure how she's involved in what's happened, but I can guarantee I won't rest easy until I hear her voice."

Now Dave was really concerned. "Sir?"

"There was a bloodbath down in Juarez. Jorge Diaz killed Emilio Rojas's oldest son and Rojas's contingent retaliated by destroying everyone related to Diaz, including Diaz, himself. The only member still living is an old woman in the last stages of Alzheimer's. I guess Rojas decided she was already as good as dead."

"How does Sonora figure in this?" Dave asked.

"Not sure, but Jorge Diaz was one of the top men in the Garcia cartel. What you don't know is that the tips we've had on Garcia's whereabouts in the States came directly from Diaz, himself, and Rojas used to be old man Garcia's right hand man. We're thinking that Diaz figured out who ratted him out and sent word to do him in."

"Talk about overkill," Dave said. "So, what do you want us to do?"

"As soon as Sonora calls, I'll let her know what's happened. I still want her to come in. We can't protect her if we don't know where she is, but I don't think she's going to change her mind. So…I'm sending out another half dozen men. They'll rendezvous with your team sometime this afternoon. Fill them in on everything you know so far and step up the search for Garcia. I wouldn't have thought it was possible, but whatever's going on with him has gotten uglier."

"Yes, sir. Will do."

Mynton disconnected just as a waitress came by Dave's table.

"More coffee?" she asked.

"Yeah, why not?" Dave muttered. "May be my last chance to get the good stuff for some time to come."

Chapter 13

Sonora woke up to a room filled with sunlight, a cup of hot coffee on the table beside the bed, and Charlie curled up on her feet.

She stretched, careful not to dislodge Charlie's comfort zone and then scooted backward until she could feel the headboard against her spine. Once she was settled, she crossed her feet, pulled the sheet up to her waist and reached for the coffee.

Sensing the possibility of a good head scratch, Charlie abandoned his spot at the foot of the bed for Sonora's lap.

"Hey, baby," she said softly. She started to pick him up, then remembered his wounds and allowed him to find his own place.

Once the cat was through moving, she took a grateful sip of coffee and laid her hand on Charlie's head. At that point, he started to purr. It sounded a little bit like an old man's snore, which made her smile. Then Adam walked into the room wearing a pair of red gym shorts and nothing else, and her smile got even wider.

"Good morning, Adam."

"Good morning to you, too, sunshine," he said softly, then frowned at his cat. "Hey, Charlie, so this is where you got off to, and here I thought you were my friend."

Adam was carrying a cup of coffee and a plate of sweet rolls. He sat down at the foot of the bed beside Sonora and then laid the plate between them.

"Help yourself," he offered, as he took a big bite of a bear claw, eyeing his cat as he chewed. "So. I let you in because I feel sorry for you, and this is how you repay me? By getting into bed with my woman?"

Sonora was grinning and couldn't stop. Not only was it charming the way Adam and Charlie communicated, but he'd referred to her as *his* woman. If someone would have asked her before she ever met Adam Two Eagles, she would have said she didn't like possessive men, but hearing those words coming out of his mouth had changed her tune. When it came to him, she liked being claimed.

She eyed the plate he'd put down, then reached for a jelly doughnut.

"Umm, my kind of man," she said, as she took a big bite.

Adam grinned. "Besides knowing how to rock your world, exactly what kind of man would that be?"

Sonora arched an eyebrow then threw back her head and laughed. Out loud. Until she gave herself the hiccups.

Hic.

"The kind of man who thinks breakfast consists of sugar," she said.

Hic.

"Take a drink of coffee," Adam suggested.

Hic.

"I didn't know coffee would cure hiccups."

Hic. Sip.

"I don't know that it will. It was just the first thing that came to my mind," he said, and took another bite of his bear claw.

Hic. Sip.

"You're a piece of work, Two Eagles," Sonora said, then began to hold her breath.

"That won't work either," Adam said, stuffed the rest of his bear claw in his mouth, chewed, then swallowed.

He was considering a second sweet roll when he saw Charlie look toward the window. A pair of robins lit on the bird feeder outside and began to feed.

Adam saw Charlie's eyes suddenly cross and his tail twitch. He recognized the signs of an imminent attack.

"Uh…Sonora, watch out. I think Charlie—"

Charlie launched himself from her lap, which meant digging in to her legs with his back claws for better leverage.

Sonora gasped in pain. Coffee lurched from one side of the cup to the other. And since her fingers had tightened instinctively on the cup handle, the fingers on her other hand—the one holding the jelly doughnut—tightened as well. Jelly squished out both ends of the roll. The south end of the doughnut squirted onto her breasts while the north end ran between her fingers and started down her elbow.

"Oh Lord," she cried, and looked to Adam for help, which was a mistake.

Adam was laughing so hard he couldn't move, let alone help. So she sat there in disgust with jelly running down between her breasts as well as down the inside of her forearm while Charlie hit the window with a thud.

It was the surprised look on the cat's face as he got up from the floor that sent them both into a second wave of hysteria. Meanwhile, Charlie stalked out of the room with his tail in the air and his ears flat to his head, indicating his total disgust with a pair of tricky birds and two humans.

"Oh my God…that was funny," Sonora said, as she tried to catch her breath. "Did you see Charlie's face when the birds flew away? It was such a…so close and yet so far away…look."

Adam's laughter had come and gone far quicker than hers. The moment he'd seen that jelly begin to slide past her breasts, he'd been unable to think of anything else but tasting it. He took the doughnut from her hand, then moved it along with the plate of sweet rolls to the floor, took the coffee cup out of her hands and set it aside, then grabbed her by the ankles and pulled until she was flat on her back.

"Adam, I'm going to get jelly all over the—"

He licked the jelly from her arm, then from between her fingers with slow, deep strokes until her toes curled.

"Uh, um…" Her body went weak. "Have mercy," she whispered.

Now he was on his hands and knees above her. Sonora saw his head dip, felt his hair brushing against her skin as his tongue licked the jelly trail between her breasts. When he started up her body to the point of impact, her eyes rolled back in her head.

"Oh. My. God."

It was her last conscious thought.

After a shower and then dressing in yesterday's clothes, which were now clean and dry, Sonora had to face the fact that her time with Adam was coming to an end. She didn't know what to think about how quickly he'd gotten under her skin. She was way more than in lust and it made her nervous.

She'd followed Adam outside and was watching him load up his pickup truck with an assortment of tools. The yard was covered with leaves and small bits of tree limbs. There was a corner of the roof off the barn and a tree had fallen across a fence. The blessing of it all was that the house had weathered it well.

"Don't you want me to help clean all this up?" she asked, as she followed him into a shed.

"No, honey. I'll tend to this after I get back." Then he picked up a chain saw and a plastic fuel can with fuel for the saw, and carried them out.

"Why do you need this chain saw?" she asked, as he set it in the truck bed up against the cab.

"In case there are still some trees blocking roads."

"Oh."

"I called Franklin while you were in the shower," Adam said. "Told him we'd be there before noon."

"Is he all right?" Sonora asked.

Adam hesitated, then nodded. "Yes, although his voice sounded weak. He may be having a bad day."

Sonora looked away. It still broke her heart to think that her time with her father was going to be so short. They were being cheated and there was nothing either one could do about it.

"So, are you ready to go?" she asked.

Adam glanced up. Sonora's eyes were shimmering with tears. That was something he couldn't bear.

"Come here, honey," he said softly, and opened his arms. She walked into them willingly and selfishly let herself be held.

"I'm so sorry that your reunion with your father has to be colored with his health crisis."

"Me, too," she said, then lifted her head and took the kiss that he offered, savoring the smell of soap on his skin.

Finally, it was Sonora who pulled back.

"We'd better go. I've left Dad alone too long as it is."

"He's used to coping alone. He's been alone all his life," Adam said.

"As have I," she said.

"Yes, but you're not anymore. Remember that," Adam said.

"Only I don't know how long I'll have him, Adam. That's what makes me sad."

Adam combed his fingers through her hair, then cupped the backside of her hips and pulled her close against him. "I'm still here," he said. "And I'm not going anywhere."

Sonora looked at him then, accepting his quiet reminder as truth. "I'm just beginning to realize what that means," she said, and then looked away. "So, we'd better get going, okay?"

Adam watched her climb into the truck and then followed her into the cab. Once she'd settled, he patted her on the leg.

"It's going to be all right."

Then he started the engine.

Sonora watched as he backed up and then started down the driveway to the main road.

"Adam?"

"Yeah?"

"When you said that it was going to be all right…"

"Yeah?"

"Well, did you know that because it's something you… uh…'know', or did you say that because it was a kind thing to say?"

He was surprised by her perception and had to think about it for a bit.

"You know what, honey?"

"What?" Sonora asked.

"I'm not really sure."

She sighed, then nodded. "Yeah. Me either," she said, then added, "But I want it to be true. I so want it to be true."

The wren Franklin had been freeing from the chunk of wood had flown out last night and landed on a nest with two tiny eggs in it.

Franklin was more than pleased with the finished product and had carried it around the house all morning, studying it for flaws. So far, he'd found none.

Finally, he'd set it on the table in front of him while he'd eaten breakfast, admiring the cocky tilt to the little bird's head.

"Little Mother," he said softly, and rubbed the curve of her tiny head, feeling the grooves where he'd given her feathers, and imagined he could almost feel a heartbeat. "That's what I'm going to call you. Little Mother."

Even though he knew it couldn't happen, he thought he heard the beginnings of a pleased chirp.

He ate his breakfast without tasting it, knowing it was important so that he could keep up his strength, and was glad for the diversion when he heard the sound of a vehicle coming down the drive.

He got up quickly and carried his dirty dishes to the sink, then started toward the front door. Before he could get there, the door opened and Sonora and Adam entered. His heart quickened at the sight of her face. If he could live one hundred years, it would still not be long enough to take her presence for granted.

He shook Adam's hand and hugged his daughter.

"So glad you're both all right. That storm was a nasty one. I'm so glad no one got hurt."

"Oh, Charlie did, but he survived," Sonora said.

Franklin frowned. "Who's Charlie?"

Adam's eyes were twinkling, although he managed not to grin. "My cat," he said.

Franklin nodded. "Oh yes. The big one with gray and black stripes."

"That's the one," Adam said.

"But he's all right?" Franklin asked.

"He had some cuts on his side and he was so cold and wet, but Adam doctored him and he was obviously well enough to attack a window this morning, trying to catch two birds at the feeder outside," Sonora said, and then grinned, remembering the sight.

Franklin chuckled, and resisted the urge to hug Sonora again. He didn't want to put her off by smothering her with attention, but she filled his heart with such joy.

As they were talking, Sonora heard the sound of her cell phone ringing down the hall.

"Oh yes," Franklin said. "Your phone. It's been ringing off and on since last night."

Sonora frowned. That didn't sound good.

"I'll check the messages," she said. "Be right back."

"Go ahead," Adam said. "I'll still be here. I want to talk to Franklin a bit."

Sonora nodded, then flew down the hall toward her room.

Once she was gone, Adam straightened his shoulders and looked Franklin in the face.

"I'm falling in love with her," he said quietly.

Franklin was not unhappy to hear it.

"What about her feelings?" Franklin asked.

Adam shrugged. "I can't tell for sure. She holds everything back."

Franklin sat down on the sofa. Adam followed.

"She's been so hurt by life," Franklin said.

Adam hesitated, then realized that Franklin needed to know what he'd seen in his vision.

"She's in danger," Adam said softly.

Franklin stilled. "And you know this because?"

"I saw it," Adam said.

Franklin's shoulders slumped. He didn't have Adam's gifts, but he knew enough to trust them.

"Does she know?" Franklin asked.

"No, I didn't tell her about the vision, but it's nothing she doesn't already know. Remember…she's the one who told us when her friend was murdered."

"What can we do?" Franklin asked.

Adam thought of the vision again, and of the helplessness he'd felt at not being able to help her.

"I don't think there's anything we can do, except trust Sonora to be able to take care of herself. There is a great power within her. More than even she knows about herself."

Franklin nodded. "Then so be it," he said.

Unaware of that she'd become the topic of their conversation, Sonora burst into her room and grabbed her cell phone from the charger just as it rang again.

She answered, a little breathless and a little nervous. "Hello."

Gerald Mynton stopped pacing and dropped into his chair with a huge sigh of relief. "Thank God," he muttered. "Where the hell have you been? I told you to stay in touch."

"Good to hear from you, too," Sonora said. "As for

where I've been…in a cellar dodging tornadoes, then at a friend's house until daylight."

"Good Lord!" Mynton said. "Real tornadoes…as in— on the ground and sucking up everything in its path?"

"As in," Sonora said, and then quickly changed the subject. "What's happened?"

"A big mess down in Juarez. Don't know how Garcia figures into it, and not sure how it impacts you, but I'm guessing it does."

She dropped down onto the side of the bed and leaned forward with her head in her hand. "Talk to me," she said.

"You know who Emilio Rojas is?"

She thought a minute, then remembered the background info on the Garcia clan. "Wasn't he the old man Garcia's right hand man?"

"That's the one," Mynton said.

"So, what does he have to do with all of this?"

"Okay, here's what we know so far. Jorge Diaz is the man who leaked info to the DEA regarding Garcia's whereabouts. We're guessing that he wanted Garcia out of the way to take over the cartel's business. With Juanito dead and Enrique already in jail awaiting trial, Miguel was the only one left in his way."

"But how did Rojas and Diaz connect?"

"We're guessing that Miguel called in a marker, talked Rojas into doing a little payback for him, and it all backfired. Diaz killed Rojas's oldest son. Rojas retaliated by decimating the entire Diaz family, except for an old woman with Alzheimer's disease."

"Oh Lord," Sonora said. "What a mess."

"That's an understatement, Jordan."

"So, how does this affect me?"

"Not sure, but there is the possibility that when Garcia

finds out what's happened, he's going to freak and blame you for the entire incident, since Juanito's death was what started this whole thing."

"Crap."

Mynton sighed. "And then some. Please. Reconsider. Come back to Phoenix where we can protect you."

Sonora thought of all that had happened to her since she'd begun this journey—the visions she'd had—the dreams of her childhood—the tattoo on her back—and Adam Two Eagles's power to heal. She didn't know what was going to happen, but she knew that whatever came, she would be safer within the boundaries of this world.

"No. I'm not leaving. I'm safe here."

"But for how long?" Mynton argued.

"Until I'm not, I guess. And when that happens, I'll deal with it, just like I've dealt with everything else. I'm not helpless, sir. The government trained me well."

Mynton leaned back in his chair and closed his eyes. "I never said you were helpless, Sonora. You're a good agent. I just don't want to lose you, that's all."

"Agents are a dime a dozen, sir, but there's only one of me."

Mynton flinched. She'd put him in his place and rightly so.

"I didn't mean that you were valuable only as an agent and I'm sorry it came out like that."

"I have a father, sir. I have never been able to say that before. He's not well and I'm not leaving him. With him, I have found where I came from, and to whom I belong. I'm not Latino, I'm Native American. I never knew that before. Can you understand what that means to me?"

"Coming from a huge Irish family, I can only imagine what it must have been like to grow up like you did. I'm happy for you, Sonora, but at the same time, you need to remember the caliber of the man who's looking for you. He's scum. Be careful…and stay in touch."

"Yes, I will, and thank you for the update."

"I don't suppose you'd be willing to meet with Dave Wills?"

She frowned. "We have nothing to talk about. Just tell him to get Garcia off my tail. In a way, it's his fault this whole mess even happened."

"Yes. I'm well aware of his foul-up in Mexico. However, what's done is done. I'll pass on your message."

"Thank you," Sonora said, and disconnected.

She sat for a few moments, absorbing the ramifications of what she'd just learned. While it was a terrible disaster for those two families, she couldn't see how it changed her situation. Garcia was still out there, looking for her. She needed to get her mind back on that and quit worrying about her new feelings for Adam. Still, as she got up to leave the room, she knew that was going to be easier said than done.

It wasn't until she reached the end of the hall that she realized her dad and Adam had moved into the kitchen. Just hearing the deep rumble of Adam's voice put a knot in her stomach. The man was magic all right, especially in bed. She was out of her mind crazy about him and unsure what to do about it.

She was still smiling as she started into the kitchen, but the smile quickly ended when she overheard the end of their conversation.

"Still no word on any donors?" Adam asked.

Franklin shook his head. "No, and they warned me early on that there probably wouldn't be. It's difficult to find a match. For whatever reasons, there are not a lot of Native Americans in the donor system and some of the markers needed for a match are confined to that specific ethnicity."

Sonora had stopped in the doorway, and now grabbed on to the wall for support. She was stunned and so mad she was shaking.

"What the hell are you two talking about?" she asked.

Both men wore equally guilty expressions as they looked up.

Adam frowned. She was angry and he couldn't blame her, but it hadn't been his story to tell.

Franklin held out his hands. "Come here, daughter. Sit with us a bit."

"I'm not sitting anywhere until you start talking. Did I hear you correctly? Are you waiting for some kind of organ donation?"

"Not an organ, exactly," Franklin said.

"Then what?"

"Bone marrow."

She reeled as if she'd been slapped. "And why wasn't I told of this? I'm your daughter. What if I'm a match?"

"This is between you two," Adam said.

For once, Sonora agreed and fixed Franklin with an angry glare. "I'm waiting," she said.

"Look. I didn't even know you existed. It was just a dream and a gut feeling that even led me to believe your mother had been pregnant with my child when she left. I was so stunned when you showed up that it never even entered my mind. Then later, when I did think of it, it didn't matter."

"Didn't matter? Didn't matter? What? You don't think it's important that I have my father around?"

Franklin sighed, then sat down. "I'm sorry. I didn't think of it like that."

Sonora's shoulders slumped. Her anger dissipated as quickly as it had come. She crossed the room and then put her arms around his neck and hugged him.

"Dad...Daddy...for God's sake. Let me be tested. Maybe this is why all of this is happening, you know? You needed me as much as I've needed you."

Franklin looked up at Adam. "If I called my doctor, could you get her to Tulsa to the Cancer Center to be tested?"

"Of course," Adam said.

Sonora unwound herself from Franklin's neck and stepped back. "Then it's settled?" she asked.

"Yes. It's settled," Franklin said.

"Good."

Adam could tell she was satisfied with the end results of the conversation, but he could tell there was still something wrong. Then he remembered the phone calls.

"Sonora."

"Yes?"

"What's happened? Is there news about the man who killed your friend?"

She looked pale, but her voice never wavered. "In a roundabout fashion, I guess there is."

"So?" Franklin asked, urging her to tell.

"It's sort of complicated, but the short version of what's happened is that two Mexican families that sort of belong to the Garcia cartel went to war. A man named Rojas was killed by another named Diaz. The old man of the Rojas family retaliated by destroying every single member of the Diaz family, including women and children."

"Dear Lord," Franklin said, and stared at Sonora in disbelief. That she could talk about this so dispassionately told him how hardened she'd become by that world.

"How does this affect you?" Adam asked.

She shrugged. "Maybe it does. Maybe it doesn't."

"What did your boss say?" he asked.

She looked up then, meeting his gaze straight on. "That everything began to come undone for Miguel Garcia when I killed his brother Juanito, and that if he blames me for that, then he might blame me for the implosion that's occurring within the cartel now."

"Which means you're in more danger than ever?" Franklin asked.

"Don't worry, Dad," Sonora said. "I'm well-trained in protecting myself. I'll make sure this ugly part of my world does not infringe upon you."

"That's not what I'm worrying about," Franklin said.

"Me, either," Adam added.

"I can take care of myself," she said, and then turned around and walked out of the room.

Adam saw the stiff set to her shoulders and the quick, angry motion in her stride, then remembered the tattoo on her spine and knew she was right. She had even more power than she knew.

Chapter 14

The drive to Tulsa went faster than Sonora would have believed. When Adam told her that it was at least a two and a half hour drive, she'd resigned herself to a long trip. But she hadn't counted on her growing connection to Adam. After the night of the storm and the passion of their lovemaking, she had been a little embarrassed about being alone with him again. However, instead of the stilted conversation she'd expected, she'd been at ease from the first. Adam even had her laughing about their passionate lovemaking by telling her that from now on, whenever he knew she was coming over, he was planning on blowing some fuses. But it was when he offered to have Charlie declawed if she would let him lick more grape jelly off her breasts, that she lost it.

Adam knew Sonora was a little nervous about what being a bone marrow donor entailed, so he'd done his best to keep her mind off of the process, and at his own expense. He grinned when she began to laugh, then returned his attention to the highway and the traffic.

She didn't know that he lived for the times he could make her happy.

He didn't know how he was going to live when the day came that she would leave.

After another hour of driving and talking, they began to approach the city.

"Is this Tulsa?" Sonora asked.

"No, it's Glenpool, but we're not far away."

"Okay," Sonora said, and then pulled at the hem of her shirt and flicked a bit of lint off her jeans.

"Are you afraid?" Adam asked.

"Not like you mean," she said. "I am afraid I won't be a match."

Adam sighed. There wasn't anything he could say to make her feel better about any of this. There was nothing to do but wait and see.

Miguel Garcia was sick of staying holed up in the Tulsa motel. He'd been trying to call the four men who'd been helping him search for the better part of thirty-six hours, but with no luck. He couldn't figure out what was going on and why they didn't answer. His only option was to call Rojas and see what the hell was going on. He knew Rojas was unhappy with what was happening, but it couldn't be helped. It was his duty, as the eldest son, to avenge his brother's death any way he could.

As he started toward the table to get his cell phone, someone knocked on his door.

"Maid service!" a woman called.

"Dios," he muttered. *"Una momento."*

He grabbed his leather vest and put it on over the sleeve-less T-shirt he was wearing, buckled the western-style belt around his waist, rubbed the dust off the toes of his boots, grabbed his phone and his hat, and stepped out of the room.

The maid slipped in behind him carrying a handful of clean linens and began stripping the bed as he got into his car. As soon as he'd turned on the engine and started the air conditioner to cool off the car, he reached for his phone. Time to make that call.

He punched in the numbers by memory then counted the rings. It wasn't until it had rung the sixth time with no answer that he began to be concerned. There was always someone at home at the Rojas estate. Maids, houseboys or any number of Emilio's large family were always coming or going. The house was never empty.

He disconnected, then tried again, thinking he might have hit a wrong number. Again, it began to ring, and again, the fifth, then sixth, then seventh ring came and went. Miguel was about to hang up when he heard some-one pick up.

"*¡Hola! ¡Hola!* Hello? Hello?" Miguel said.

Emilio Rojas took a slow breath. "Yes. I am here," he said.

Miguel's concerns faded. "I've been calling and calling. Where the hell is everybody?"

"We've been to a funeral," Emilio said.

Miguel frowned. "Oh. Sorry. Anyone I know?"

"My oldest son, Emilio Jr."

Miguel grunted as if he'd been punched. "What happened? Was it an accident?"

"No. It was murder."

"Murder? Who did it? I will make them pay!"

Rage rose so fast and so high in Emilio's chest that he thought he would explode.

"Who did it? Who did it? I did it, that's who. I sent him to run your little…errand…and this was the result."

Rojas had never spoken to Miguel in this tone of voice—ever.

"I didn't think…I mean, I never intended for—"

"It is of no importance anymore," Emilio said softly. "They are dead. All of them."

Miguel stuttered, then choked.

"They?"

"The Diaz family. Who else?" Emilio said.

Miguel had visions of wives, mothers, children, brothers and sons. There had been a lot of them—at least twenty-five or thirty and Rojas had—

Madre de Dios.

"I'm sorry," Miguel said. "I didn't know—"

"You are on your own," Emilio said. "I have called in my men. They are no longer doing your dirty work for you. Do not call me again. Ever. Do not come back to Juarez. Do not even come back to Mexico. If you do, I will know it, and I will kill you, myself."

The line went dead in Miguel's ear.

Time passed, but Miguel couldn't have attested to the fact. He still had the phone to his ear when someone wheeled into the parking space beside him and gunned the engine. As it revved, it backfired.

Miguel flinched and ducked. The phone went flying.

It was a few moments before he realized he was still breathing and that he hadn't been shot at. Just the victim of a car in need of new plugs and points.

He got up from the seat, muscles trembling and gasping for breath. Everything he knew was gone. It no longer mattered if Jorge Diaz was dead or not. With Emilio Rojas for an enemy, his days were numbered.

He rubbed the palms of his hands on top of his head, feeling the faint stubble of new growth and realized he needed a shave. His fingers were trembling as he swiped them across his face. Then he doubled up his fists and began pounding the steering wheel. He didn't know he was crying until he felt the tears on his face, and even then, couldn't think past the rage.

Everything was fine until the DEA messed in his business. Sonora Jordan had been the agent who killed Juanito. She represented everything he hated, and if it was the last thing he did, he was going to wrap his hands around her neck and watch the life go out of her eyes.

Sonora was white-lipped and shaking when she came out of the doctor's office, but it wasn't entirely from pain. The stress of knowing she was her father's only chance to live was taking its toll. When she saw Adam stand up and start toward her, her eyes welled with tears. She hated this weak-kneed, sissy side of herself—hadn't even known it existed until she'd met Adam Two Eagles.

"Are you all right?" Adam asked.

"I'm just peachy," she said, and ducked her head to hide her tears.

"I already saw them so get over it," Adam said, as he handed her his handkerchief.

"God. Can't even shed a few tears without you getting all bossy about it."

Adam sighed. It figured she'd rather make an ass of herself than let someone see her cry. Damned if that didn't endear her to him even more.

"It's not about being bossy, Sonora. It's because I care about you and you know it."

She rolled her eyes, thumped him on the arm in frustration and then hugged him.

"You cheated," she muttered, wincing as she walked.

He smiled gently as he helped her out the door.

"How did I cheat?" he asked.

"You're too nice. It's impossible to be mad at nice."

He grinned. "Well, that's something I've never been accused of before, and if it will make you feel any better, there's a whole company of Army Rangers who would disagree with you."

"So, tough guy, take me home."

Adam frowned as he watched her walk. Her normal stride was gone and she was moving gingerly, as if there was a pain in her back.

"Are you in much pain?"

"It wasn't great," she muttered, remembering the punch of bone marrow they'd taken from her right hip.

"Did they give you some pain medicine?"

"Yeah. Shot me full of the stuff and gave me some to take home."

"Then we should go before it wears off," Adam said. "You can eat as I drive, then sleep if you wish."

Miguel had made up his mind. He was going to go back to Phoenix and wait for Sonora Jordan to surface. She couldn't stay on the run forever. The way he figured it, when she walked in her front door, she'd get a welcome she never expected and he'd get the justice he deserved. Still, to be on the safe side, he was going back in a different car.

He'd been at the used car lot for almost an hour, waiting for the salesman to get the okay from his boss on the money Miguel wanted for his black Jeep.

The sun was hot, which matched his mood. It was long

past noon and he wanted food and something cold to drink. Just as he was about to go into the office to look for the salesman, he saw him coming out. He was smiling, which bode well for Miguel. Miguel was guessing that he was about to get the price he'd wanted, which meant he would have more than enough money to buy the other car he intended to use for the trip back to Phoenix. Since his money sources had been cut off, he didn't have money to waste.

As he was standing in the lot, there was a sudden squeal of tires and several horns began to honk. Someone cursed and another cursed back.

Miguel turned to look.

The driver of a car and the driver of a delivery truck had just had a fender bender. Traffic was stalling in both directions. He was thanking his lucky stars that he wasn't out on the street in the middle of the mess when he noticed a dark-colored pickup truck about three vehicles back.

He saw the long-haired, dark-skinned man behind the wheel and marked him as Native American, but it was the woman sitting in the seat beside him that made his heart skip a beat. He stared in disbelief.

It couldn't be.

He scrambled in his wallet for the photo of Sonora Jordan that he'd been carrying, then compared it to the woman in the truck. It was her! It had to be—either that or a double.

He stuffed the picture back in his wallet and then started to run.

"Hey! Hey, mister!" the salesman yelled. "What about your money?"

Miguel hesitated, then turned around.

"I'll be right back," he shouted, and then turned back toward the street.

The truck was still there, but a couple of police cars had

arrived and traffic was beginning to move. He cleared the curb in a leap, and without care for the traffic, started running toward the truck.

"Do you think anyone was hurt?" Sonora asked, as she scooted to the edge of the seat to get a better look at the wreck.

"I think they're yelling too loud to be very hurt," Adam said.

"Yeah, you're right, and for that I am glad. I hate this kind of stuff. Never would have made a good patrol cop."

"I disagree," Adam said. "I think you would be great at anything you set your mind to doing."

Joy settled in Sonora's heart. She could get spoiled with this positive affirmation Franklin and Adam seemed bent on giving her.

She saw movement from the corner of her eye as she leaned back in the seat and turned to look. Some bald-headed cowboy had come running out of a used car lot and was headed toward the accident.

"Look at that nut," Sonora said. "He isn't paying any attention to the traffic."

No sooner had she said it than someone on a motorcycle, thinking he could bypass the traffic jam by winding through the stalled cars, came flying out from between two vehicles and hit the man in mid-stride.

"Oh no!" Sonora gasped, and flinched as the man flew up into the air and then came down on his back. It was instinct that had her reaching for the door handle when Adam grabbed her arm.

"No, honey. Police are already on the scene, as are a couple of ambulances. If you get involved, then you'll have to identify yourself, and that might not be such a good idea."

She sighed, then let go of the door.

"You're right. I just wasn't thinking."

At that point, traffic started to move. Sonora stared out the window at the injured man, and winced. She could see blood coming out of his nose and ears, which was never a good sign. Head injuries were tricky. She hoped that he would be all right.

Lunch had come and gone a few days later, and Franklin was sitting in his favorite chair out on the back porch, watching a pair of bluebirds taking turns feeding the babies in their nest. In the middle of his meditation, he heard the phone ring. Frowning, he started to get up, then remembered Sonora was inside and sat back down.

The male bluebird seemed to be on watch duty as his mate darted from the nest up in the branches to the ground below, then back up again. He could just see the edge of the nest and the open beaks of her three babies, begging for whatever it was she brought back. It pleased him to see these tiny moments with Mother Earth and her children, and wouldn't let himself dwell on the fact that one day he would be gone and life would go on without him.

Sonora hadn't spoken one word about the bone marrow testing since her return from Tulsa, and he hadn't asked her. He knew she was scared. He also knew that she feared she would fail him. He didn't have the words to comfort her, because the truth was, for the first time in months, he had hope and it was because of her. In the beginning, even though he didn't want to die, he'd come to terms with it. But now that he knew he had a daughter, his acceptance of death had done a one-eighty change. Truth was, he didn't want to leave her or this earth.

The screen door opened behind him. He heard the hinges

squeak, then the loud pop as it slammed shut. He turned around. Sonora was coming toward him, and she was crying.

His stomach rolled. Something terrible must have happened.

In a panic, he stood up and started toward her, then she started to laugh through her tears.

"Dad…I'm a match! Your doctor wants you in the hospital tomorrow before noon. Says they have to prepare you for the transplant…whatever that means."

Franklin was taken aback, both by the news and the suddenness. He'd been going to take Sonora and Adam to the pow-wow. Obviously, that was going to have to wait.

He wanted to laugh, to dance, to clap his hands and run in circles. Instead, he took her by the shoulders.

"It will not be pleasant. Are you sure you want to do this?"

"Absolutely positive," she said.

It was then that he laughed. "This is, indeed, the most wonderful news."

Sonora wrapped her arms around his waist. "It's going to work. I can feel it in my bones."

Franklin silently agreed. Considering the power that was within his daughter, he had no doubt that her healthy blood cells would not only heal him, but make him as good as new.

"Little woman of the snake," Franklin whispered.

Sonora heard and shivered. She hadn't considered the significance of her snake and the Kiowa beliefs in power and healing, but it was obvious Franklin did. She didn't care what they believed as long as her father got well.

"Do you mind if I leave for a bit? I want to tell Adam, but not over the phone."

"Of course, but you're welcome to take my car."

"Thanks, but I have a need to feel the wind in my hair."

Franklin eyed the dark wings of hair framing her face and recognized the restlessness of her spirit.

"Ride safely," he said.

She nodded, absently, then looked up at Franklin. "Do you think he'll come with us tomorrow?"

"I think wild horses couldn't keep him away," Franklin said.

Adam had just returned home after a visit to an elderly couple from the tribe. Daisy, the wife, had a bad case of poison ivy from gathering mushrooms. While it was rare that Native American people contracted poison ivy, it did happen. The entire time he was treating her, she kept blaming her grandmother's predilection for sleeping with white men as the reason she had succumbed to the rash.

In her own words, "Indians don't get poison ivy. It's the taint of white man's blood that weakens my body."

Adam knew she was miserable, and that her opinion of white people was normally just fine. But it was the itching and swelling all over her face and arms that had her in such a bad mood. He'd left her with salve and kind words, and a suggestion to her husband to do the cooking for a while so Daisy wouldn't be exposed to the heat.

He'd been in the house long enough to put up his bag of salves when he heard the familiar sound of a motorcycle coming down the drive. He spun toward the sound.

Sonora!

He went out to the porch. The sound was getting louder. Within moments he saw her flying toward him, barely outrunning the cloud of red dust behind her.

Sonora's heart jumped when she came around the bend in the road and saw Adam waiting for her out on the porch.

She couldn't wait to tell him—to see the joy in his eyes. She rode into the yard and then stopped abruptly, turning the bike in a quick half-circle before dropping the kickstand and killing the engine. She hung her helmet on the handlebars then dismounted quickly, unaware of Adam's silent admiration.

"What a nice surprise!" Adam said, as he met her at the steps.

"You have no idea," Sonora said. "I have news. Good news. I'm a perfect match to be Dad's donor."

Adam grinned and picked her up in his arms and gave her a ferocious hug.

Sonora laughed when he turned them both in a circle, then did a little two-step.

"That's phenomenal!" he cried. "Come in. Come in. Tell me what the doctor said."

She followed him inside, then into the kitchen. She began to talk as he poured them both cold drinks. "I have to have Dad there in the morning before noon. The doctor said there are some things that must be done before surgery can occur. Something about isolation and irradiating him. They have to kill his bad cells and his good cells, too, before replacing them with some of mine, or something like that. I was just so excited at the news that only parts of it soaked in."

Adam handed her a glass of cold Pepsi, then sat down at the table across from her.

"Yes, I'm familiar with it. All of that must be done before they put your healthy bone marrow into his body."

"Yes…that's it," Sonora said.

"Would you let me drive the both of you back to Tulsa?"

Sonora smiled. "I was hoping you'd say that."

Adam reached across the table and took her hand. "We're in this together, okay?"

The smile on her face disappeared as she nodded and looked away.

"Did I say something wrong?" Adam asked.

She hesitated, then made herself look up. He was always honest with her. She could do no less.

"No. Quite the opposite."

He frowned. "I don't understand."

"I've never been part of a 'we'. It's always been a 'me', and I'm not complaining. It just touches me, that's all."

Adam's heart tugged. Over and over, he was struck by the loneliness that had been her life until now. Even though he was moved, knowing that she valued his presence in her life, he wanted her happy, not constantly reminded of her past.

"So…you like being touched, do you?" He pulled on her fingers, spreading them wide, then threading his fingers through hers. "I'd be happy to oblige with more touching—in private."

Sonora grinned. "Subtlety is not one of your strong suits, is it?"

Adam pretended dismay. "Ah, lady…you wound me by doubting my intentions."

"Your intentions weren't to get me in bed?"

"Well…yes…but you would have enjoyed it, too."

This time when she laughed out loud, he grinned.

Chapter 15

Franklin's pulse was rapid. He knew it. The nurse knew it and gave him a studied look, as if trying to judge the reason.

"When did you take your last dose of medicine, Mr. Blue Cat?"

"This morning, as directed."

She nodded and made a note.

"Once we start the irradiating process, you will be in isolation, and will continue to be isolated after the transplant until you are released."

"Yes, I am aware of the restrictions," Franklin said. "However, the possibility of being cured far outweighs the aggravation."

She smiled. "Yes, sir. You are so right."

"May I see my daughter now?"

"Yes, of course. I'll send her in."

Franklin leaned back in the bed, grateful for a few moments of respite. The trip had been wearing, and the hustle and fuss of getting admitted, then changing out of his clothes and into hospital clothes, as well as all the lab work that occurs upon admission had tired him.

He hadn't expected to be reluctant to leave home, but once the time had come, he realized there was a chance he might never come back. Surgery was a chancy thing at best, and Franklin was not at his best. He had accepted the possibility of not waking up once the transplant began, but still had pangs of sadness as he locked the door to his home and then left. However, once they'd begun the journey, his attitude had changed to one of hope. Now all he had to do was maintain positive thinking and trust the process.

His eyes were closed and his breathing was steady when he felt a touch on his hand. He looked up, then he smiled.

"Hello, daughter."

Sonora leaned over the bed and hugged, then kissed her father.

"I don't want you to stay alone at the house," he said.

"Of course, I will. There's nothing—"

His fingers curled around her wrist.

"Please. Adam already suggested it and I completely agree. Your situation is not a normal one and you know it. How can I rest and heal knowing your life might be in danger? Besides, within a few days the surgery will happen and you do not need to try and heal from your part of it all alone."

Sonora hadn't thought this far ahead, but obviously Franklin and Adam had.

"All right, Dad. I promise."

"Good," he said, and when she would have pulled away, he still held her. "There's something else you need to know. I have changed my will. You are my sole heir. Even if I don't survive this illness, you still belong to the tribe and to our land."

Sonora's eyes teared. "I don't want to talk about—"

"I don't either, but one must face the inevitability of mortality. No one lives forever."

Sonora pulled up a chair and sat down, then leaned forward and laid her head on the bed near where Franklin lay. He reached for her, laying his hand on her head. They stayed that way until finally a nurse returned. After that, the visits were over.

"I'll see you in surgery," Franklin said.

"Count on it," Sonora said, and gave him a big thumbs up and a smile as she left.

She made it all the way down the hall to the waiting room, but when she saw Adam's face, she began to cry. He went to her, comforting her as best he could, but there was little he could do. Right now, everything was out of their hands.

Just twelve doors down the hall was Miguel Garcia. He'd been in a coma in Intensive Care ever since he'd been brought to St. Francis. His head injury had been severe, resulting in a considerable amount of swelling on his brain. For a few days it had been touch and go, but somewhere around midnight last night, he had started to turn a corner. He'd quit struggling for breath and had shown signs of increased brain activity. Garcia woke up slowly, uncertain of where he was or how he'd gotten there. The nurse who was checking his vitals noticed that he was coming around and quickly rang for the doctor.

Miguel groaned.

The nurse moved to his side. "Mr. Trujillio, don't move, okay?"

He groaned again. Who the hell was Trujillio?

"You're in a hospital. You were hit by a man on a motorcycle. Do you remember?"

Images came and went so fast he couldn't assimilate. He was in an English-speaking hospital, which meant he must be in the States, but he couldn't remember why or how he got here. He wanted to tell the nurse to call his brothers, but the words wouldn't come.

Moments later, a doctor strode into the room, but it was too late for questions. Miguel was out again.

Adam stopped by Franklin Blue Cat's home long enough for Sonora to pack her belongings. She didn't have much and it didn't take her long, but as she was going through the house to make sure everything was turned off and locked up, she saw the carving of her kitten and put it inside her bag.

"I think I have everything," Sonora said, as she walked back into the living room where Adam waited. He'd already loaded her Harley into the back of his truck, and there was nothing to do now but leave.

"If not, you're welcome to anything that's mine," he said.

Sonora nodded as she started toward the door.

Suddenly, the room tilted and disappeared. The strap on her bag slid off her shoulder and hit the floor, but she didn't hear it, or Adam's sudden call of concern.

She was alone and in the dark and she didn't know what was wrong with her, but knew she was either sick or injured. She was weak and frightened, and at a level she'd never known. The air was filled with the sound of gourd rattles, from behind her—in front of her—on both sides of her—and there were voices. She'd never heard the voices before. They were speaking in a language she'd never heard, and yet somehow, she knew what was being said.

This was a warning of danger. Not imminent, but danger still the same.

Then just as quickly as it had come, it was gone. When she would have staggered backward, Adam caught her. The moment she felt his arms around her, she went weak.

"Sonora…what the hell just happened to you? Are you ill?"

"Just like before," she muttered, and covered her face with her hands.

Adam grabbed her hands and pulled them away. "Look at me!" he said.

She moaned. "Sonora! Talk to me, damn it! What do you mean, just like before?"

She shuddered as she made herself focus. "It was some kind of…hallucination. I've been having them since the day the Garcia arrests went bust."

"It's not a hallucination…it's a vision. Tell me what you saw."

"Lord…I'm not sure what I saw and what's part of my imagination."

"Just talk to me," Adam said.

"Everything was dark. I was weak, either from an injury or illness, I couldn't tell, but I wasn't myself. I didn't see anything, but I knew I wasn't alone. Then the rattles started. The sound was all around me, and out of that, I heard voices, only they weren't speaking in English. It was a language I didn't understand, but I knew what they were telling me."

Despite the fact that Adam completely believed in what she was saying, it was unsettling to know what she was going through.

"You said, they. There was more than one voice?"

She frowned. "I didn't realize it until you just pointed

it out, but, yes, there was more than one voice, only they were telling me the same thing."

"The Old Ones," Adam muttered, more to himself than to her. "You said you knew what they were saying?"

"Sort of. I can't explain it, but somehow I did."

"What was it, honey? What were they telling you?"

"That my life is in danger—not imminent, but it's coming and I must be prepared."

Adam grabbed the bag that she dropped and then took her by the hand. "Come on. We're leaving now."

"What's the hurry?" she said. "I told you that the danger wasn't imminent...or at least I don't think so."

"I want to get you settled and then put you in protection."

"I'm not going to be locked up, so don't even go there," she said.

"I'm not talking about walls you can see."

In the back of her mind, she heard one last, distant rattle, as if reminding her to heed. She shivered.

"What kind of protection are you talking about then...some spell like the one you say brought me here?"

"I'm not talking about anything. Just get in the truck," he said shortly.

She did.

Miguel Garcia had been suffering from a fever for the past two days. His sleep had been restless and broken, and when he did sleep, his dreams were crazy and disjointed. But the evening Franklin Blue Cat had been admitted to the hospital to begin the process that might give him a new chance at life, Garcia woke from his sleep with a cry of dismay. The fever had broken, and so had his heart. He'd dreamed his brother Juanito was dead, and when he woke, remembered that it wasn't a dream.

On the heels of that revelation, he also remembered why he was in the States.

Sonora Jordan.

He'd seen her.

She'd been right within his reach and then the accident had happened. Once again, bad things had come to him because of her. Without thinking of the consequences, he sat up and started to swing his legs off the bed. It was fortunate for Miguel that the nurses always kept the guard rails up because the moment his head came off the pillow and he tried to sit up, he had no sense of balance.

His upper body lolled sideways, then slid at an angle off the side of the bed. Pain lanced through his shoulders and up the back of his head. He was trying to grab hold of the guard rail when the door to his room flew open. Two nurses grabbed him just before he fell over the side of the bed.

"Get his arms!" one of the nurses shouted, as she rang for more help.

Before Miguel knew what was happening, he was flat on his back in the bed with his arms strapped down.

"No! No!" he kept screaming. "You don't understand! I have to get up. I have to find her!"

He was still shouting when a nurse rushed in and shot a syringe full of sedative into his IV. He felt the onrush of unconsciousness, even while he was still screaming.

Sonora's stay with Adam was strained. She kept jumping at shadows and was afraid to go to sleep at night. Adam had lights on all over the house for reassurance, which meant no one was getting much sleep. Charlie sensed the discord and abandoned the both of them for the peace and quiet under the back porch.

She'd called Mynton twice in the last two days to see if

there was any new news regarding Garcia's whereabouts, but all Mynton could tell her was that everything had gone quiet. The powers that be had even ordered Dave Wills and the other DEA agents to be called in and assigned to other, more pressing business.

Sonora had accepted the news without comment, but when she hung up the last time, she knew she wouldn't call again. They'd abandoned her to her fate.

Then the phone call came from Franklin's doctor at St. Francis. The transplant surgery was scheduled. Sonora was to come in before noon tomorrow and the surgery would be the day after that.

Adam gave her the news with a piece of pie and a Coke, then sat down beside her while she ate, waiting for her to say what she needed to get said.

"I'm going to miss you," he said.

Sonora was scared, and because she felt completely off kilter, she picked on the only person around who was on her side.

"You're either a masochist or a liar. I've been nothing but a problem to you and Dad ever since the day of my arrival. I'd think you'd be happy to get your life back," she snapped.

He frowned.

"Well…I'd tell you that I didn't have much of a life until you rode in on that damned Harley, but since I'm supposed to be a liar, I don't suppose you'd believe that."

His sarcasm wasn't lost on Sonora. She stared down at the plate and the half-eaten piece of pie, then sighed and set it aside.

"I'm sorry."

"You should be," he said shortly. "I don't know anything

more to say to make you believe that I care for you." Then he laughed, but the sound wasn't happy, just resigned. "I can tell you for sure that loving you is a lonely damn job."

The words were like a slap in the face. She looked up at him as if she'd never seen him, then leaned back in the chair.

"You love me."

"Is that a question or a statement of disbelief?" he asked.

Her chin quivered, but she lifted her head proudly. "Why?" she asked.

"Damned if I know," Adam said. "I never thought of myself as a masochist, but I must be. Every time you throw another log onto the wall you keep between us, I keep knocking it down and climbing back over."

His words hurt. She'd never been on this side of his anger before, and it didn't feel good. The only problem was, she was the one who'd put herself here.

"I'm sorry," she muttered.

"Why? Because I love you, or because you don't love me? Either way, don't worry about it."

She reeled as if she'd been slapped. The room was filled with anger, and she didn't know where it had come from. One minute she'd been eating pie and the next thing she'd done was pick a fight with the only man she'd ever let herself care about.

She got up from the chair, walked out of the kitchen, got the keys to her Harley, and walked out of the house.

She could hear Adam banging dishes in the kitchen as she threw her leg over the bike and picked up the helmet. Part of her wanted to ride with the wind in her hair and to hell with safeguards, but she had family to consider. If something happened to her, Franklin's second chance at life was over before it began. So she pulled the helmet down onto her head and fastened the strap under her chin.

The engine turned over and then caught. Sonora revved the engine once, then twice, then shoved the kickstand up with the heel of her boot and took off.

Rocks and dust flew out behind her as she spun out of the yard and headed down the driveway. She didn't know where she was going, but she had to get away. Too much had happened in too short a time. She'd been alone too many years and had no idea of how to accept something freely given, like love.

Adam heard the engine start, and for a moment, thought about racing out and stopping her. But he made himself stay, and when he heard her riding away, he threw the dishcloth into the sink and walked out of the house in the other direction. Either she'd come back or she wouldn't. Either she'd love him or she couldn't. There was no power on earth, or from the Old Ones, that could stop what was already turning.

Sonora rode with a stiff-lipped concentration that would have made Gerald Mynton proud. This was the agent he knew and counted on—the woman who was more machine than human. Only she wasn't running away any longer. She was riding back to Adam as fast as the bike would take her. She wouldn't let herself think of the oncoming night. She'd ridden in the dark plenty of times before. She'd had stake-outs in the dark, too. There was nothing in the dark that was so different from the day. Just less light to see it by. But coming in to a dark house was another thing altogether. That's where she'd been locked up as a child, and that's where the ghosts of her past still lived.

When she finally saw the dirt road leading from the highway up the mountain to Adam's house, she breathed easier. She hadn't meant to go so far so fast. She'd just needed some fresh air.

Now, here she was, only minutes away from Adam and she couldn't wait to get there. She only hoped that he could forgive her for being such an ass. She took the turn without slowing down and accelerated as the bike hit dirt. One mile, then a little bit more and she would be there.

She didn't realize until she took the last turn that she'd been holding her breath. But when she saw that every light in the house had been left on for her, she exhaled quickly, then choked on a sob.

She came to a sliding halt, then when she tried to stand, all but fell on her face. Her legs were weak and shaking as she tore off the helmet and then tossed her hair, reveling in the night air blowing through the length. She hung her helmet on the handlebars and started toward the porch, her steps dragging. It wasn't until she reached the front door that she realized she wasn't alone.

Adam had been sitting on the porch, waiting for her to come back long before night had fallen. He couldn't believe that she was still out in the dark, and didn't know that, for her, there was a fine line between a dark house and a dark night. He didn't know about the closet or the men who'd paraded through her foster mother's life.

He hadn't realized until he'd heard the Harley's engine, that he'd been bracing himself for a disappointment. The relief that came with the sound was huge, and as he sat in the dark, listening to her coming closer and closer, he fought the urge to cry. She made him weak in ways he would never have believed, and yet he loved her with a strength of passion that surprised him.

Then she was here, getting off the Harley, and tossing that wild mane of hair that had been shoved up under the helmet. He saw her face in the faint lights coming through the windows and knew she was as lost as he felt. Her shoulders were slumped as she started up the steps. When he saw her wipe a weary hand across her face, he couldn't stand it any longer. He shoved the chair out from under him as he stood.

"Adam?"

He stepped into the light.

She paused.

He kept walking until they were face to face, then he took her in his arms.

"I'm sorry," he said softly.

"So am I," she countered.

"Come inside with me?"

"Yes," she whispered, and leaned against his strength.

He kissed her then, felt the tremble in her lips as he tasted dust and tears.

"Come lay with me, love. I will hold you while you sleep."

She let herself be led because she was too weary to remind him that he, too, had been missing sleep.

Later, she stood beneath the shower head as warm water sprayed down upon her body and let him wash her as if she was a baby. Afterward, he dried her hair, then her skin, and pulled back the covers of the bed.

"Get in, honey," he said gently. "I'll be right back."

She crawled beneath the sheets, then rolled over on her side as Adam made a last check through the house to make sure everything was locked. Only after he crawled into bed beside her and pulled her safe against his body did she trust herself to close her eyes.

"Adam…"

"Sssh," he said softly. "Go to sleep."

Silence filled the room, then Adam became aware of the

sounds of the house. The slight drip of the shower head, the sound of wind rising, the pop and creak of the older house as it, too, settled for the night.

Finally, he shut his eyes. Just between consciousness and exhaustion, he thought he heard Sonora speak, then he convinced himself he must have been dreaming, because he thought he heard her say that she loved him.

The surgery was successful.

It was the first thing the doctor told Adam when he entered the waiting room. Adam grabbed the doctor's hand and then shook it, from one healer to another, although the doctor would have argued the point.

"When can I see her?" Adam asked, referring to Sonora.

"As soon as she comes out of recovery. Franklin, of course, is already in isolation in ICU. He will not be having visitors."

"I understand," Adam said. "How soon will we know if the transplant worked?"

"Soon," the doctor said. "Blood tests will tell us a lot in the next few days. But you have to trust the process and that all takes time."

"If Ms. Jordan's recovery is normal, how soon before she can go home?" Adam asked.

"Will she be on her own?" the doctor asked.

"No. She'll be staying with me until she's back on her feet."

The doctor nodded. "Then I'd say probably tomorrow or the next day. We want to make sure she's in no danger of infection and regaining her strength. As for the visit now, I'll have a nurse let you know when she's back in her room."

"Thank you," Adam said. "Thank you more than you will ever know."

The doctor smiled. "It's been my pleasure, believe me."

With that, he moved on to the next surgery awaiting him, while Adam sat back down and waited to see Sonora.

About forty-five minutes later, a nurse came looking for him. "Adam Two Eagles?"

Adam stood. "Yes, ma'am?"

"Come with me," she said.

He followed anxiously.

Sonora was back in her bed when he entered her room. She was pale and too quiet for his peace of mind. He walked to the edge of the bed, then laid a hand on her forehead, instinctively feeling for fever. At his touch, she moaned.

"Adam?" she mumbled.

He leaned close and kissed the side of her face. "I'm here," he said softly. "It's over. You did well and so did Franklin. Close your eyes and sleep, love. I'll be here when you wake up."

She meant to ask him something else, but between one breath and another, she forgot. The remnant of the anesthesia was still in her system and quietly pulled her under.

She woke three more times, but for less than a minute, before falling back to sleep. It was some time in the night before she woke up for real, and when she did, saw Adam asleep in the chair beside her bed. His presence was proof of his faithfulness. He'd promised her he would be there for her, and he was. Satisfied that all was right with her world, she managed to roll over onto the side opposite the one where the bone marrow had been taken. Once she was at ease, she fell back to sleep.

Two days later, Miguel was out of restraints, but they kept him sedated more than he liked. Upon complaining, his doctor had explained the reasoning for the treatment and the problems of confusion that often came with head injuries. It made enough sense that Miguel hadn't argued, but he was counting the days until he could get out and resume the hunt. He'd seen her once. He would find her again.

He judged the time and the days by the number of times nurses changed shifts. He'd also learned that the nurses who came on in the afternoon and stayed until midnight were the ones who talked the most. This evening was no exception. One had carried in his food on a tray while another was administering medicine through his IV. He watched as the clear liquid left the syringe and went straight into the drip.

"Will this put me to sleep before I get a chance to eat my food?" he asked.

"It's not a sedative," the nurse said. "It was an antibiotic, but if they're serving meatloaf for dinner this evening, you might wish you'd slept through it."

Her laughter sounded like a cackling hen. When she slapped her leg and then added that she'd been teasing, he didn't smile. There was nothing funny about any of this.

The other nurse, who Miguel thought of as a busybody, took the lid off the food tray and set it on the table then swung it over Miguel's bed.

"Can you manage?" she asked.

"Yes," he said, and picked up the enclosed packet that held plastic cutlery and condiments.

The two nurses were talking to each other as they finished their work in his room. At first, he paid no attention until he heard one of them mention a name.

"It's like something out of a Hollywood movie," Cackling Hen said. "Imagine, finding out you have a daughter and then having that daughter save your life."

"I know," Busybody said, then lowered her voice. "I heard she's some kind of government agent."

Cackling Hen nodded. "Yes, so did I." Then she

frowned. "I wouldn't take that kind of job if you gave it to me. I mean…everyone knows that people who's jobs take them undercover have to do things with the bad guys to keep from being found out. Imagine having to have sex with some drug dealer or murderer?"

Busybody snorted. "Lord, Carleen, aren't those kind of people one and the same?"

Cackling Hen laughed and then shrugged. "Yes, I guess you're right."

However, Miguel wasn't laughing. When he'd heard the words, "she", then, "government agent", his attention had shifted. Still, there had to be plenty of people who worked for the government in Oklahoma. Just because he was looking for one, didn't mean they had to be one and the same. Still, he couldn't help but ask.

"So…you say a woman saved her father's life by donating an organ?"

"Not an organ. Bone marrow," Cackling Hen said. "Quite a story. And the father's famous."

Miguel lost interest. To the best of his knowledge, Sonora Jordan had no family and he would certainly have known if she had famous parents.

"Hmm," he said, and salted the green beans on his plate.

"Ooh, really?" Busybody said. "I didn't know that."

"Apparently, they didn't know each other existed until a short while ago. It's just like a movie, I tell you."

"What's he famous for?" Busybody asked.

"He carves things out of wood, but a lot of Native Americans are good at art and stuff."

Miguel stilled. Native American? The woman he was looking for could pass for a Native American.

Busybody wasn't through with her interrogation. "What's his name?" she asked.

"Franklin Blue Cat," Cackling Hen said. "He lives up in the Kiamichi mountains. Has a studio there and ships his work all over. I heard some Japanese big shot even commissioned some work from his once."

"Never heard of him," Busybody said, then added, "I'll bet he's rich, though."

"Yeah, and can you imagine what the long lost daughter must think? Not only has she found a family, but the family is rolling in dough. What are the odds of that?"

"So, this Blue Cat woman works for the government. They have good benefits and all. My Al tried to get on a government job, but he didn't have the right credentials," Busybody added.

"Her name isn't Blue Cat. Her last name is Jordan."

Miguel knocked over the glass of iced tea on his tray, which sent both nurses scrambling to mop up the spill. One left to get him a refill, while the other went to get a clean sheet while Miguel accepted what fate had dropped into his lap. If he was to believe his luck, the woman he sought was here in this hospital. He already knew that this wasn't the time or the place to exact revenge, but at least he knew his search was over. He had a name and a place to start looking.

Chapter 16

Sonora was packed and ready to go, and none too soon for her. She'd had all of St. Francis Hospital that she cared to experience. Whoever said that a hospital was a good place to heal had never tried to sleep in one. Now all she had to do was wait for Adam to arrive. The drive home would be long and most likely uncomfortable for her, but the end of the line promised peace and quiet and Adam's loving arms, which was worth whatever it took to get there.

She glanced at the clock, and then out the window. It was too early for Adam to get here, but she didn't feel like sitting any longer. She got up and headed for the door. At least she could take a couple of turns around the floor. The sooner she recovered her strength, the better off she would be. She hadn't forgotten her last vision, or the warning she'd had of coming danger and she wanted to be on familiar ground if it happened.

Even as she was stepping into the hallway, the hair rose on the backs of her arms. It was a warning she'd heeded many times before, and to her advantage. But this time, although she was without her weapon, felt she was surely safe. After all, it was broad daylight and there were people everywhere. Her warning had been about darkness.

She stayed close to the handrail on the side of the walls in case she had a moment of lightheadedness or felt sick, but it didn't happen. In fact, the farther she walked, the better she felt. The doctor had assured her that as long as she didn't overdo it, she would be back to normal in no time.

She had walked all the way to the end of the hall and was about to turn the corner when she was awash in cold air. The faint sound of rattles sent her grabbing onto the handrail for fear another vision was imminent and that she might fall. But the world didn't shift and the hallway didn't disappear. And when she looked up, she realized she was standing beneath an air conditioner vent.

Disgusted with herself for jumping to conclusions, she continued her walk, right past the half-open doorway where Miguel Garcia lay watching television. He didn't see her. She didn't see him, and even if she had, wouldn't have recognized him as anyone except the man she'd seen getting hit. Without his mustache and hair, he was a stranger.

By the time she circled the hall and was back to her room, she was shaky. She stretched out on her bed and closed her eyes, and when she next woke, Adam was standing beside her bed.

"Hey, pretty lady," he said softly, and kissed her on the cheek.

She smiled and then turned her face just enough so that the kiss settled on her lips instead.

"Mmm, good," she said softly, when he pulled away. "I am so ready to go, but there's some paperwork that—"

"Already tended to," he said. "All you need is the wheel-chair, and that's coming up."

"Then we can go?"

"Yes, honey, we can go."

"Did you see Dad?" Sonora asked.

"Only through a window. He's not allowed visitors, remember?"

She nodded. "Did he see you?"

"Yes. He waved…once for me, once for you."

A bright smile spread across her face. "He did that?" she asked.

"Yes, baby…he did that."

After that, Sonora was satisfied and within minutes, they were gone from the floor.

The trip home wore Sonora out. Adam had reclined her seat in the truck and within an hour of leaving Tulsa, she was sound asleep. She slept all the way to Adam's home, then managed to get inside before she crawled into bed again. Adam helped her off with her clothes, and once she was comfortable, he pulled the covers up over her shoulders, pulled down the shades at the windows, and left her alone so that she could sleep.

The phone rang several times during the rest of the day, but Sonora barely heard it. Adam was fielding requests from some of his patients, wanting everything from his advice to some kind of healing. Because he wouldn't leave Sonora alone, he dispensed advice over the phone and requested the sick to come to him. There was a room in his house that he had set aside for times such as this, and so he waited as they came and went.

And so the day went, and each ensuing day afterward

until Sonora was almost one hundred percent back to her old self and Adam wasn't so concerned about leaving her on her own from time to time.

Sonora talked on the phone to her father on a daily basis, and with each passing day it became evident that Franklin Blue Cat had a new lease on life.

It seemed, to Sonora, that the world was, once again, spinning properly on its axis, and whatever danger that had once awaited her was gone. In her mind, she spun several scenarios, all of which had Miguel Garcia either dead or on the run. She hadn't thought past Franklin coming home from the hospital and had told Mynton that she was considering an early retirement. He was understanding, but regretted her decision and kept telling her not to make any hasty decisions.

However, it was Adam's constant and faithful presence in her life, and the family unit that he and Franklin represented, that appealed to her most. Bottom line, she was in love with Adam Two Eagles and if there was a snowball's chance in hell that he returned the feelings enough to keep her around for the rest of her life, she wasn't going anywhere.

Miguel was being dismissed. Days earlier, when his memory had returned, he'd had the foresight to call the used car dealer. The salesperson was relieved to hear Miguel's voice, assured him that they still wanted to buy his car, and that the money they had agreed upon earlier was still good. He'd come to the hospital that same day with the luggage that had been in Miguel's car, the papers Miguel needed to sign, and a cashier's check for the car that he'd sold. Now, he had just enough money from selling his car to pay for his hospital stay, which left him flat broke but upright and still determined to exact revenge.

The hell of it was, he had millions in a Mexican bank and even more in an offshore bank in the Cayman Islands. Any money he might request to be transferred from the Mexican bank would certainly pinpoint his presence to the authorities. But there was a chance that they didn't know about the Cayman accounts and he needed money. It was a risk he was going to have to take.

Even though he felt weak and shaky, he was on his own. He took a cab to a motel, got a room and dumped off his luggage, then headed for one of the larger downtown banks.

He filled out the necessary paperwork to access a transfer to the new account he'd just opened, and asked how long it would take.

The banker, being the sympathetic man that he was, had already learned of Miguel's plight. He remembered hearing on the news of the incident where Miguel had been hurt, so he did all he could to facilitate a quick response. Within twenty minutes of a phone call, then a corroborating fax with the proper account numbers, over half a million dollars had been transferred into Miguel's new account.

He was all smiles and charm as he withdrew a hundred thousand with the explanation that he would be buying a new vehicle and didn't want to run short, then left the bank. He hailed another cab, went back to his motel, and slept for the better part of eleven hours. When he woke up, he was starving and it was three o'clock in the morning.

He called a cab, which took him to an all-night diner. He ate ravenously, hailed another cab back to the motel, and slept until after ten the next morning. It was then that he ventured out to the car dealers, paid cash for a brand new car and drove off the lot feeling much better about himself.

After a few wrong turns, he found his way to the Tulsa

library, parked and went in. Playing upon the sympathy of a middle-aged female librarian who obviously viewed his accent as romantic, she helped him get online and straight to a Web site devoted to wood carver and sculptor, Franklin Blue Cat, which included the area in which he lived as well as a business number.

He jotted them down and left while the librarian was busy tending to someone else, stopped to buy gas and an Oklahoma road map, then went back to his motel.

He studied the map for the better part of the day, located the Kiamichi mountains and the town nearest where Franklin Blue Cat supposedly lived, and then took a long nap. He was conserving energy for the day when revenge would be his.

He was there for two days before he decided it was time to make his move. He longed for his native Mexico, but knew that as long as Emilio Rojas lived, he could never go home. However, there was always the Caymans. A large part of his money was there, and once in residence, he could have his account in the Mexican bank transferred, as well. Yes, it was a plan that suited him, and he longed to begin his new life. But there was a piece of his old one that had yet to be dealt with. Once he knew that Sonora Jordan was as dead as his Juanito, then he would start over and not a day before.

It was a hundred and three degrees in the shade. Sonora knew because she could see the reading on the outdoor thermometer Adam had hung on the porch. It was cool in the house, but confining, and Sonora itched to be outside, doing something. She felt as if she was in hiding, even though most of her indoor activities had been in place because of the need for rest and healing, rather than a reluctance to show herself.

Adam had gone to visit an elderly woman who wanted him to give her a potion to get a man for her granddaughter, who had been living with her for five years. She told Adam that her granddaughter was lazy and getting fat and if she didn't find a man and get married soon, no one would have her.

Adam had stifled a grin and told her that he would certainly stop by on his way into town. She didn't know it and he wasn't going to tell her as yet, but he wasn't going to pretend, like some healers he knew of, that there was such a thing that could be concocted. What it amounted to was a young woman with no self-confidence and a grandmother who wanted her little house back to herself.

He'd left Sonora with the number to his cell phone and a promise of bringing home some ice cream along with the groceries. He'd gone so far in planning ahead as to having an ice chest in the truck to keep the refrigerated and frozen items from spoiling on the way home.

Sonora thought of the shaded creek below the house and the cool running water. It wouldn't be much over her ankles, but it was out of the house and something different to do. Excited now that she had a plan, she went to change into some shorts instead of the jeans she was wearing, and tennis shoes instead of bare feet. She eyed the small, healed wound where the bone marrow had been removed. There was no more pain or stiffness at the site, and deemed it to be fit. She thought about taking her cell phone, then discarded the notion, left Adam a note telling him where she'd gone, and then hurried out the back door.

The heat was like a slap in the face. There was a moment when she thought about changing her mind and going back into the house, but the creek wasn't far and the thought of walking barefoot in the water was too enticing to ignore.

A few minutes later she was on the bank above the creek. She saw the sweat lodge but left it alone. It had nothing to do with her and she didn't want to intrude in a place where she didn't belong.

She looked down at the creek, and as she'd expected, the water was running free and clear. From where she was standing, she could see a crawdad as well as a couple of small frogs moving about in the water below. The trees on both sides of the bank leaned slightly toward the water, their branches forming an arch above it. Pleased with herself for thinking of this, she found a way down that wasn't too steep, and once on the narrow shore, took off her shoes and stepped in. Compared to the temperature of the day, the water was cold, but it felt wonderful.

There were small rocks along the sandy bottom that had long ago lost their jagged edges by the constant flow of sand and water. A squirrel immediately voiced its disgust at her unexpected appearance and promptly dropped a couple of acorns near where she was walking, as if to scare her away. She looked up just in time to see a little red squirrel disappearing into the upper branches.

"Everyone's a critic," she said, and proceeded to wade along the creek bed.

She came upon a small, deep pool about three feet in diameter and paused to look down. As she did, a tiny green snake that had been lying on some nearby rocks made a quick getaway by slithering off into some leaves.

Sonora felt a moment of recognition with the little snake as she thought of the one on her back. In a moment of abandon, she stripped off her shirt and shorts, leaving her in nothing but a pair of bikini panties, then folded them up and left them lying on a pair of flat rocks at the edge of the shore. She checked her wound again to make sure it was not getting dirty or wet, and then straightened.

The sway of hair hanging down her back and the air on her body was a sensual experience she hadn't expected. But for the narrow strip of turquoise silk that passed for underwear, she was naked as the day she'd been born, and loving it.

A pair of hummingbirds darted past her line of vision on their way up from the creek where they'd been getting a drink. She watched until they reached the top of the bank, then began drinking nectar from the red-orange trumpet flowers hanging from their vines among the trees. For a brief, fanciful moment, she could almost envision what life had been like for her people many, many, years ago, when their only concerns had been finding food and shelter from one season to the next.

She lost all track of time down in her little Eden, and was crouched down and staring into a round hole in the creek bank when she heard a twig snap on the banks above her.

Startled, she straightened, and for the first time, realized the danger of being down here alone and naked.

"Who's there?" she called out.

At that point, Adam appeared on the bank above. He'd been going to tease her for slipping off to the creek like a child, but when he saw her, the words died on his lips. There wasn't one child-like thing about the woman standing in the water.

She was golden-brown all over, with curves that could make a man weep. She was holding her hands over her breasts until she saw it was him. At that point she dropped them to wave a hello and he almost fell into the creek.

"You're a little overdressed," Sonora said, and then laughed softly, as if she knew a secret he didn't know.

"Yes, I can see that," he said, and then jumped from the bank down to the shore without bothering to find a good place to descend.

"Don't hurry on my account," Sonora said, and grinned.

But the smile slid off her face when Adam began to undress.

"Uh…"

He didn't take his gaze from her face as he came out of his shirt, pants and shoes. Unlike her, he didn't stop with the underwear. Before she knew what was happening, he was completely nude.

His long brown body and hair dark as night made him look like a savage, then her gaze shifted to his face. She took a deep breath, and then sighed.

"You are so beautiful," she said softly. "Did you know that?"

He walked into the water and came toward her.

Her eyes widened as she realized his intent. She laughed as she spun, and started to run, splashing diamond-like droplets of water as she went.

Adam hesitated only once when she turned her back. He saw the snake. It certainly wasn't the first time he'd seen her naked with the tattoo completely revealed, but it never failed to make his heart skip a beat. But after that, the hesitation was brief as he bolted after her.

He caught her in three strides, spun her around and yanked her close against his chest.

"You're supposed to be recuperating."

She leaned her head back against his forearm and stared straight into his eyes. She could feel every curve and muscle in his body, as well as his breath against her face. His eyes were dark and glittering with a warning she didn't mistake.

"Recuperating?" she repeated.

He nodded.

She slid her arms up around his neck. "So heal me," she challenged.

Before she knew what was happening, he had stripped the bit of silk from her hips, lifted her off her feet, and with his hands under her backside to guide the way, lowered her down onto his erection.

Sonora moaned beneath her breath as he slowly filled her, then closed her eyes.

"Does this hurt you?" he asked.

"Lord, no," Sonora said.

"Then open your eyes and know the man who loves you."

Sonora did as he asked, locked her legs around his waist, and her arms around his neck, then held on as he took her for a ride.

At that point, everything seemed to happen in moments of slow motion.

A ray of sunlight coming down through an opening in the limbs that settled on the crown of his head.

The sound of flesh against flesh as Adam took her where they stood.

Droplets of water on Adam's face mingling with tiny beads of sweat.

His nostrils flaring.

Her breasts pressed against his chest as the ache between her legs blossomed, then exploded in a blinding white light of passion.

As she was coming down from the adrenaline rush of her climax, she felt Adam shudder. Before she knew what was happening, his hold on her tightened. One more thrust, then another and he suddenly threw back his head and let go with a groan.

It echoed up and down the creek bed, startling a small fox out of hiding and sending a pair of doves flying from the branches of a tree above them.

As the last bird took flight from the creek, Adam gently set her back down, then took his hands and proceeded to wash them both from the clear, running water of the little creek.

Sonora steadied herself by putting both hands on his shoulders as he knelt at her feet, washing her gently with water he cupped in his hands.

His hair was silky to the touch, his shoulders broad and strong. She said his name, just to hear it from her lips.

"Adam."

He paused, then looked up.

"I think there's something about me you should know," she said.

He straightened, then waited.

"I'm going to tell you something that I've never told another man. Ever."

His heart thudded once out of rhythm.

"I'm in love with you," she said. "And it scares me to death."

Relief hit him like a fist to the gut. He combed his fingers through her hair, then pulled her to him, his voice husky and full of emotion.

"I had begun to fear I would never hear those words from your lips. I love you, back, Sonora, more than you can imagine. I want to know that I will see your smile each morning and feel your hands upon me every night. I can't even face the thought of a life without you."

"You don't have to," Sonora said, and gave herself up to his kiss.

Adam held her there, in the middle of the creek with the

water running cool on their feet and the trees shading their bodies from the sun, and knew that for the rest of his life, he would forever associate this place with her.

Finally, he urged her out of the water, helped her dress, then dressed himself. He showed her an easy way up from the creek, then together they walked back to the house.

Sonora was so happy and at peace that she didn't even heed the faint sound of running horses, or the distant gourd rattles in the back of her mind. She was too full of Adam and the love they'd just professed.

Miguel had been up and down every road within a fifteen mile radius of Franklin Blue Cat's home and gallery, and that was after realizing that no one was home. He cursed himself for not thinking to check at the hospital before he left to see if anyone knew who'd taken Sonora Jordan home. It was obvious she was not in residence at her father's home, but considering the fact that she'd been part of some transplant procedure, he was assuming she might have needed aftercare. At that point, he remembered the Native American man she'd been with, and the dark blue Ford truck he'd been driving and figured if he could find that man, he might find Sonora.

He'd thought about going back down the mountain to the small town he'd passed through before going to the Blue Cat gallery, then decided against it. He didn't want anyone remembering later that a Latino man had been asking about the woman, especially when she later turned up dead. He'd given himself permission to do a little investigating on his own, then worry about being recognized later.

He'd driven for what seemed like hours without seeing anything resembling that truck, and then he'd taken a corner in the two-lane dirt road a little too wide and found himself almost face to face with the truck and the driver he'd been looking for.

He swerved immediately to the side to avoid the head-on collision and shrugged and waved, hoping that it passed for enough of an apology that the bastard didn't stop and start a fight. He was feeling okay, but he definitely did not want to take a blow to the face.

He saw the man nod and wave back, and breathed a quick sigh of relief. Noting the direction in which he was driving, he waited until the dust was almost settled, then followed. It didn't take long to see the little road leading up the mountain that the Native American had taken. He stopped for a moment, trying to decide if he wanted to chance being seen again, or wait until dark.

But the area was new to him, and the mountain was heavily wooded. He didn't want to play detective in the dark with a bunch of coyotes, so he took a chance and followed.

Within a couple of minutes, he realized this was a driveway, and not another main road. He parked and started walking, taking care to stay within the edge of the trees. Before long, he saw the roof of a house. After a couple more minutes of walking, he saw a house, then the pickup itself, although no one was in sight.

He was just about to go back to his car when he saw the man come out of the house and head toward the backside of the property. Miguel watched until he disappeared, then proceeded the rest of the way up the drive. If someone else was in the house when he knocked, he would pretend he was looking for Blue Cat's gallery and got lost. And if no one else was there, it wouldn't take him long to check out the place, just in case.

When he reached the front door and knocked, no one answered. He smiled to himself and reached for the doorknob, thinking he might force the door, only to find out that it turned beneath his touch. His smile widened. Rural people who still didn't lock their doors. He couldn't believe his luck.

He glanced quickly toward the direction that the Native American had gone, and then stepped inside. He knew within seconds of entering that there was no one there. It felt empty, as if the energy of the place had departed with the occupants.

Careful of the time, he made a quick sweep through the house to reassure himself that he was alone, then did a second run-through of the bedrooms. Only one bedroom seemed to be occupied, but there were things belonging to two people. As he looked out a back window, he saw the back end of a motorcycle sticking out of a shed. He looked closer, and when he saw the Arizona tag, smiled to himself.

He remembered she'd owned the Harley Buddy Allen had once had. So that's how she got out of town.

He thought about hiding somewhere in the house and surprising them both when they came back, then decided against it. That Native American was big and Jordan was DEA. Neither one would be easy to take down. Besides that, he wanted the woman to suffer. She wasn't going to get off so easy with a quick bullet through her head.

Having settled all of that in his mind, he hurried out of the house the same way he came in, pausing long enough to make sure there was no one in sight, then made a run for the trees.

He was breathing hard and sweating when he reached them, and could feel the beginnings of a headache. He was used to heat, but there was something different about this Oklahoma heat that sapped the strength right out of him. He wouldn't have been interested in listening to someone speak about the humidity factor in the state, but if he had, it would have soon become apparent to him what the difference was. Oklahoma in the summer was a perpetual sauna.

He stopped for a few moments to rest, and as he was waiting, saw the man suddenly appear from below the crest of a hill, only this time, he wasn't alone. He watched carefully, then started to smile.

He'd found Sonora Jordan.

Chapter 17

By sundown, what appeared to be a group of thunder clouds was gathering on the horizon. Another round of storms was evident—something they dealt with at this time of year. Adam stood out on the back porch, judging the possibility of its arrival before morning and figured it was likely.

Charlie was winding himself around Adam's legs, begging for supper.

"Okay, okay, I hear you loud and clear," Adam said, and headed toward a shelf on the back porch to get a can of cat food.

Charlie voiced his pleasure with a small, happy "mowrp" which made Adam grin.

Sonora was in the kitchen, finishing up the dishes that she'd insisted on doing, since Adam had cooked the meal. As she was hanging the dish towel up to dry, the telephone rang.

"Adam! Phone!" she called.

"Get it for me, will you?" he called back. "I'm feeding Charlie."

Sonora took the wall phone off the receiver. "Adam Two Eagles residence."

There was a single second of shock that someone other than Adam had answered, then someone started talking—fast and loud—and in Kiowa.

Sonora didn't know what was going on, but she could tell something was wrong. "Adam! Come quick!"

He dropped the empty can into the trash as he hurried into the kitchen and took the phone she thrust into his hands. Within seconds of taking the phone, he began to talk, louder and firmer, and in the same language.

Within seconds, he'd obviously gotten the caller's attention, because he began to ask questions and in English.

Finally, she heard Adam say, "I'll be right there."

Sonora could tell Adam was bothered when he hung up the phone, and when he turned around to face her, he was frowning.

"What's wrong?" she said.

"I have to go. A young man has been injured and he's also in trouble."

"I'll go with you," Sonora said.

Adam's frown deepened. "It's better if you don't."

"Why?"

"Because I'm pretty sure that the injuries he's suffered are from making meth. You're DEA. You don't want to be in the middle of this."

"Oh crap," she muttered, immediately getting the message as to what her life would be like married to Adam if she became legally involved with the people he'd come home to help.

"I'm sorry," he said. "It sounds like he needs an ambulance and to be taken to a burn unit, but they won't do a thing until I tell them it's all right."

"Why are some of your…our…people so distrustful of whites?"

He sighed, then held out his hands. "Let's just say that if you'd been raised Indian, you would probably understand."

She flinched as if she'd been slapped. "Prejudice? In this day and age?"

"Lazy. Blanket-ass. Living on tribal money and not working. I could go on and on, despite the fact that every bit of it is lies."

"Good Lord," she muttered, then waved him on. "Go. Go. Whatever has happened, they need help, but not mine. At least, not yet."

Adam hugged her quickly, thanking her in the only way he knew how, then grabbed his bag, his car keys, and headed out the door.

"Lock the door behind me!" he yelled, as he bounded off the porch.

"Wait! You forgot your phone," Sonora said, and carried it out to the truck.

He tossed it in the seat beside him as he was starting the engine. By the time Sonora got back into the house and locked the door, he was already gone.

Miguel was coming up the mountain from the town below when a pickup truck appeared at the crest of a hill and quickly sped past. He had a quick glimpse of a dark truck and then nothing. He cursed softly, hoping that he hadn't waited too long and that upon his return to the house, Sonora Jordan would be gone.

Still, he retraced the path that he'd taken earlier in the

day and almost missed the turn in the dark. He stopped, backed up, then started up the dirt road that led to the big Native American's house. When he was almost there, he turned out his lights and drove the rest of the way in the dark, guided only by a faint bit of moonlight.

He saw the lights before he saw the house, and when he saw a light suddenly go off in the back part of the house, his spirits lifted. Someone was home, most likely her. When he drove up to the house and realized the pickup was gone, he smiled.

That had been the Native American he'd met coming up.

She was home alone.

He grabbed his handgun from the glove box, then got out. As he stood there, the moonlight suddenly disappeared. He looked up. The stars were disappearing, as well. When a couple of raindrops suddenly splattered on his face, he realized a fast-moving storm was moving into the area.

He smiled.

Even better.

She wouldn't hear him coming in the wind and the rain.

He hurried up onto the porch, then did a quick check through the curtains at the windows. He couldn't see details, but he could tell there was someone inside moving around.

A loud clap of thunder suddenly slammed down upon the roof, followed by a swift flash of lightning. Miguel ducked in reflex, then swiped a shaky hand across his face. That had been close—too close.

He moved toward the front door, then gripped the knob, expecting it to turn as easily as it had earlier and was surprised that it was locked. Cursing softly beneath his breath, he started to draw back and kick down the door when it suddenly opened.

He froze momentarily at the shock of suddenly seeing Sonora Jordan only inches away.

Sonora gasped. In the half-light and despite the bald head, she saw the family resemblance. Miguel Garcia had found her.

Lightning flashed again.

The lights went out!

Dark was the impetus Sonora needed to move. She pivoted sharply and darted toward the bedroom where she kept her gun. Before she'd gone two steps, she was hit from behind in a flying tackle. The impact of Garcia's weight against the place where the bone marrow had been taken left her screaming in pain and her legs almost too numb to move.

"I will kill you, bitch! Just like I killed your friend in Phoenix. Just like you killed my little brother."

It was the mention of Buddy having been beaten to death that gave her the will she needed. Still on her belly, she bucked her body violently, as if trying to unseat a rider, then kicked out with both bare feet. She knew she'd connected to something vital when she heard the pitch of the man's scream.

She didn't know that she'd just broken his nose, or that, for the time being, he was blind with pain. All she knew was that when she got up to run, no one was stopping her.

Thunder rocked the house as the squall line hit. Sonora heard the tinkle of breaking glass and guessed that the fiercely blowing winds had probably blown something through a window. She thought of the storm shelter only a few yards away from the house. She probably needed to be down there, but she wasn't going without her gun. The last place she wanted to be was cornered and helpless.

She reached Adam's bedroom in seconds. The dense

blackness in the room was unnerving, but the fear of the man behind her was worse. She felt along the walls until she came to the closet, then yanked it open and dropped to her knees. Her bag was down here somewhere, and inside it was her gun.

She heard running footsteps now, and the wild, frantic screams and curses of a man in pain. Her fingers were shaking so badly that she couldn't even find the bag, then when she finally did, couldn't get a grip on the zipper.

The door to Adam's room hit the wall with a bang just as she found the zipper tab. She pulled frantically, then thrust her hand inside the opening. Within seconds, she had the gun. She felt along the bottom of the bag until she found the small magazine of bullets as well, and shoved it up into the grip. Under the cover of thunder, she jacked the barrel and loaded the first bullet into the chamber.

Slowly she stood, with the gun in her hand, waiting for that flash of lightning to tell her where her enemy stood. Within seconds it came. She saw Garcia at the same time he saw her. Then the room was once again dark.

Sonora fired a shot in the direction of where he'd been standing, and then kicked the door hard. There was a loud cry of pain as she dove out of the closet and onto the bedroom floor. A half second later, a shot went over her head.

She felt the edge of the bedspread against her cheek and without thinking, slid under the bed, then out the other side, bringing her closer to the door. When lightning flashed again, she saw Garcia's boots facing an opposite wall. The moment the light was gone, she jumped up and ran.

Within seconds, he was once again in pursuit. Her legs were cramping and there was a spreading pain going down the back of her hip from where he'd landed on her. Sensing that he was only a step or two behind her, she spun, firing off two shots as she did, then fell backwards into the kitchen as he ran past. With only seconds to spare, she rolled to her feet, made a dash for the kitchen door, then ran out into the storm.

Adam was within a mile of the family's residence when something moved in front of the headlights. He swerved to keep from hitting it as he slammed on the brakes. By the time he came to an abrupt halt, he was shaking.

At first, he thought it was a deer, but it had gotten away. As he started to take his foot off the brake, something began to materialize just beyond the lights. He watched in disbelief as a rider on horseback came out of the dark, then grunted, as if he'd been punched. Both rider and horse were transparent.

Nothing was said, but he heard the meaning just the same.

Go home. Go home.

Then one last word surfaced.

Hurry.

The hair rose on the back of his neck. Sonora!

He grabbed his cell phone as he turned the truck around, calling his own number. To his dismay, there was no answer, and when he began the trip home, realized he was driving into a storm.

He thought of the young man who awaited him, who was possibly dying of burns. There was nothing to do but get help. He dialed one more number—to the local fire and ambulance service.

The dispatcher answered on the first ring. "Fire and rescue, what is your emergency?"

"Travis, this is Adam Two Eagles. I got a call from the Wapkinah family up on county road 114. Their oldest boy got burned. They called me first, but I'm calling you. I can't get there and I don't want that boy to die."

Travis Younger immediately understood. "Thanks, Adam," Travis said. "We'll get 'em some help."

"Thanks," Adam said. "Talk to you later," tossed the phone into the seat beside him, then stomped on the gas.

Miguel was blind with pain and choking on his own blood. She'd broken his nose for sure—once with her foot and the second time with the closet door. He kept trying to remember the layout of the rooms he'd seen earlier in the day, but with the pain and the dark, it was confusing.

The next time the lightning flashed, he realized he was in the room all alone. It occurred to him then that he might be in trouble. He pivoted abruptly and began to retrace his steps. After the second sweep through the house, he knew she was gone.

Cursing in both English and Spanish, he stumbled through the kitchen, wiped the blood off his face with a small towel, then shoved it up against his nose, hoping to stop the flow.

He moved out onto the porch just as another flash of lightning came and went. It was then he saw his car was missing. With a scream of rage, he ran out into the storm. It took another flash of lightning and the rain in his face to realize he wasn't at the front porch, but the back.

He looked toward the shed and saw the faint outline of the Harley. She had to be somewhere nearby.

"Hear me, bitch!" he screamed. "Hear me, good. I will make you wish you'd never been born before you die."

He heard the shot too late to duck. It was nothing but luck that he was still standing when the bullet hit the porch post right behind him. He hit the ground, belly first, splattering water and mud in his mouth and up his still bleeding nose.

The roar of his rage was so loud that Sonora heard it over the storm. If the storm didn't pass too quickly, and if Adam came back in time, she might have a chance of staying alive.

She'd already been in his car and tried to hot-wire it, but the new models and safeguards that were in place made that impossible. She had an added advantage of knowing the property far better than he did and thought about hiding out in the woods. He'd never find her, but there was a part of her that feared he would give up and leave, which meant she would be facing him again sometime, and the odds might not be in her favor.

She didn't know where he was until another strike of lightning came and went and she saw him moving toward the cellar. At that point, she was glad she wasn't in it, and ran to the front of the house.

It didn't take long for her to break the valve stems off the tires. She could hear the hiss of escaping air as she stood. Then she saw him, less than five yards away, with his gun pointed right at her face.

"Drop it!" he yelled, waving his gun in her face.

"Or what?" she screamed back and took aim with her own. "You're going to shoot me anyway. I'd rather take you with me."

They both fired.

Sonora was falling backwards as the first bullet came out of her gun. It hit Garcia in the shoulder, spinning him around. The gun fell out of his hand into the mud while the bullet he'd fired plunged into the ground just beside Sonora's head. Mud and water flew into her eyes, momentarily blinding her.

For a few seconds, both Sonora and Garcia were out of

commission. She struggled to get up, while Garcia dealt with more pain and the loss of his gun. When he saw that she was down, he pounced. Bleeding from his shoulder and his nose, he went belly down on top of her. The impact knocked the wind out of Sonora's lungs and for a few frantic moments, she was paralyzed, unable to move.

In the fleeting breath between heartbeats, a gust of wind blew rain into Sonora's face. She gasped, and in doing so, drew sweet, life-giving oxygen into her body. At the same time, the air was suddenly filled with the sound of drums—and of gourd rattles—and voices chanting over and over in a language she did not know.

Garcia's hands slid around her throat.

She was fighting him and kicking and gouging at his eyes, pushing against his weight, but to no avail.

The drums grew louder as did the rattles. Sonora wondered if this was what the Kiowa heard when they were going to die.

And then suddenly, the weight was off of her body. She struggled to get up and felt hands beneath her arms, pulling her upright, but when she turned to look, there was no one there.

Garcia was standing a short distance away from her, holding his arms up across his face as if to ward off a blow, although there was nothing between them but the downpour of rain. He was screaming and praying as he'd never prayed before.

Sonora felt a great wind at her back and feared a tornado was about to drop down. She tried to move—to run for the cellar—but her feet wouldn't move. All around her, the air was filled with the beat of a thousand drums and the ground shook from the shock waves of gourd rattles and she thought that they were going to die.

Then, through the wind and the rain and the war drums hammering against her brain, she saw a flashing, bouncing light. Someone was coming up the driveway at great speed. When she recognized the pickup and the man who jumped out on the run, she screamed out his name.

"Adam!"

He launched himself at Garcia as he spun and fired. The bullet went wild as Adam hit him waist high and sent them both flying into the rain. At the moment of their impact, it was as if Sonora was suddenly released from a spell. Frantically, she began feeling about in the mud to find her gun, and just as suddenly, it was in her hand.

She turned.

Lightning flashed.

Garcia was getting away from Adam.

She fired into the air.

Then time seemed to stop.

Garcia froze with Adam still holding on to his leg.

The rain stopped.

The quiet was even more frightening than the storm.

Garcia was looking at something above Adam's head, and the look on his face was one of horror.

Sonora turned, following his line of vision, and that's when she saw them.

"Adam."

Her voice was barely above a whisper, and yet he heard it. As he turned to look, Garcia rolled away from him and grabbed his gun from the mud. He turned, firing as he rolled, willing to die if he could take her with him.

The bullets didn't find a target, but lightning did. It came out of nowhere and nailed Garcia to the ground. Fire came out of his ears and the bottoms of his feet. Within seconds he was gone.

Adam looked up.

There were four Native Americans above him, one naked and riding a pure white horse. One was wrapped in a bear skin, one wearing a war bonnet that trailed the ground, and one with a white handprint on either side of his face. They were mounted on horses with fiery red eyes and stamping feet.

The one on the white horse waved a war shield as the horse reared up, then disappeared. Another shouted something into the wind, until one by one, they were gone.

"The Old Ones," Adam said.

Sonora stumbled, then sat flat.

Adam ran toward her, then picked her up in his arms.

"When I saw you two in the headlights, I thought I was going to be too late. He had his arms around your throat. I saw you fighting him, then suddenly he went flying. You must have landed quite a blow."

The war drums were silent as were the gourd rattles. The fear that had been with her since the day she'd learned Buddy Allen was dead was no more. She felt empty and free and ready to be filled with Adam Two Eagles's love.

"It wasn't me," she said. "It was them. They saved me."

Adam shuddered, then held her closer. "Let's get in the house. You need to get cleaned up and into dry clothes, and I've got to make some calls."

Sonora suddenly remembered the boy who'd been burned. "What happened to the boy?" she asked.

"I don't know. I was almost there when one of the Old Ones stopped me. When I saw him in my headlights, I knew you were in some kind of danger. That's why I came back."

Sonora laid her head against his shoulder as he carried her inside. She'd seen them for herself, it still seemed impossible to believe. Still, Garcia was dead, which was good, and since he wasn't alive to be telling what he'd seen, then she had nothing to worry about.

Once they were inside the house, Adam lit candles for her again. She was standing in the laundry room taking off her wet, muddy, clothes when the power suddenly flickered, then returned.

Sonora breathed a sigh of relief, but not because she was no longer in the dark. She was pretty sure that the events of this night had cured what ailed her about darkness. Her greatest joy right now came from knowing she could get clean.

Adam came from the kitchen with a large bath towel. He wrapped it around her, then helped her to the bathroom.

"Need any help?" he asked.

"No. I can handle it," she said, and dropped the towel. As she turned to step into the shower, the tattoo of the snake rode the movement of her muscles, making it appear as if it were about to strike.

"You sure can," he said softly, and left her on her own.

A short while later, the front yard of Adam's house was crawling with all manner of authorities. The local sheriff, the county division of the DEA, and someone from the Feds was supposed to be on the way.

Miguel Garcia had once been a big deal in this country, responsible for funneling billions of dollars worth of drugs up from Columbia, through Mexico, and then into the States.

As far as the law was concerned, he'd attacked a DEA agent in a plot of revenge. She wounded him twice, before he succumbed to a lightning strike during a storm.

It was a good story and Sonora Jordan was sticking to it.

Epilogue

Franklin Blue Cat was sitting in his favorite chair, watching the sunset from the screened-in back porch of his home. He could hear his daughter's laughter and the deep, rumbling voice of her husband, Adam, as he responded to something she'd said.

He heard her footsteps moving across the kitchen floor and smiled to himself. She was coming to check on him, when it was she who should be sitting with her feet in the air.

"Dad, need something cold to drink?"

He shook his head, and then held out his hand. "Come to me for a moment," he said, and pulled her down in his lap.

"I'll squash you," she argued, even as she was sitting.

"That tiny baby in your belly weighs nothing," Franklin said.

"Maybe so, but tiny baby's mother weighs plenty," she argued, then flinched. "Oh! Man! That was some kick."

She splayed her hand across her belly and then rubbed, as if trying to soothe the infant within.

"Already he is impatient to be born," Franklin said, and laid his hand ever so gently on the round swell of Sonora's stomach.

Adam came out onto the porch with two cold, long-neck bottles of beer. "Here, Grandpa, something to cool your throat."

Franklin took it with a smile and then lifted it to a toast to Adam. "To your son and my grandson," he said.

Sonora frowned. "Hey, I'm in this party, too."

"Yes, but you're not drinking, little Mama," Adam said, then he lifted the bottle to her. "To Franklin Blue Cat's daughter, who just happens to be the woman of my dreams…and to Sonora, the light of my life and the mother of my son."

She beamed as both men lifted the bottles to their lips and took a long drink. She didn't care. She'd never liked beer much anyway.

Then Adam set his beer aside and lifted her out of Franklin's lap and into his arms. While Franklin watched and grinned, Adam waltzed her down the back porch and then up again.

Sonora had the world—and the men of her heart—at her feet. She'd never been happier, or more fulfilled. Her days with the DEA seemed like they'd happened to someone else. Only rarely did she ever think of the department or the people she'd known, and only then with a distant fondness. She didn't miss anything or anyone, because here she was whole.

Franklin smiled, and then leaned back in his chair and closed his eyes, letting the sounds of their joy and laughter wash over him in healing waves.

It was amazing how good he felt these days.
Remission, they called it.
He knew better.
Because of his daughter, he knew he was cured.
Only time and the Old Ones would prove him right.

* * * * *

Coming in November from

Silhouette®

INTIMATE MOMENTS™

and author

Brenda Harlen
Dangerous Passions
IM #1394

With a hit man coming after her,
beautiful Shannon Vaughn was forced to
go on the run with Michael Courtland,
the sexy P.I. assigned to protect her. But
as the enemy closed in, Shannon realized
she was in greater danger
of losing her heart....

*Don't miss this exciting story...
only from Silhouette Books.*

Available at your favorite retail outlet.

COMING NEXT MONTH

#1391 THE BLUEST EYES IN TEXAS—Marilyn Pappano
Heartbreak Canyon

Logan Marshall was on a mission to get revenge on the man who killed his parents. His only obstacle was private investigator Bailey Madison, who wanted to reunite him with his family. Bailey's offer to help bring the murderer to justice in return for Logan returning home led them to high adventure...and into each other's arms.

#1392 THIRD SIGHT—Suzanne McMinn
PAX

Anthropologist Nina Phillips's affair with D.C. cop Riley Tremaine ended in a car crash that left him near death. But a government agency secretly saved his life by implanting a chip that allowed him to witness acts of mass terrorism before they happened. When Nina's precious work became the focus of a madman's plot, Riley had no choice but to do whatever it took to keep her research secret, and protect her against all odds.

#1393 HONEYMOON WITH A STRANGER—
Frances Housden
International Affairs

Design apprentice Roxie Kincaid was mistakenly plunged into a cat-and-mouse game of international espionage. To survive she played the part of the secret agent she was thought to be while imprisoned with *actual* secret agent Mac McBride—who posed as a criminal mastermind. Could they contain their secrets and their growing passion long enough to stop a global menace?

#1394 DANGEROUS PASSIONS—Brenda Harlen

When a mobster sought vengeance against her, Shannon Vaughn was forced to go on the run with Michael Courtland, her private investigator guardian. And as her protector turned out to be an impostor sent to kidnap her, she had to trust that the real Michael would keep her safe from harm. But could Shannon put her life in the hands of a man who could easily steal her heart?

SIMCNM1005